"I won't be responsible for you!"

Chloe looked at him, startled. "Of course not!"

"I won't fight your battles for you or protect your innocence or mollycoddle you in any way!"

"I never asked—"

Gib's finger stabbed the air, making his point. "I just want it clear. If you stay, you're on your own!"

Chloe stood her ground. She even looked mutinous. He thought she might bite his finger.

"Yes, certainly!" she agreed. As he turned away, she asked almost belligerently, "Is there anything else?"

He whirled back. "Yes! You'll damned well keep your clothes on!"

ANNE McALLISTER was born in California. She spent long lazy summers daydreaming on local beaches and studying surfers, swimmers and volleyball players in an effort to find the perfect hero. She finally did—not on the beach, but in a university library where she was working. She, her husband and their four children have since moved to the Midwest. She taught, copyedited, capped deodorant bottles and ghostwrote sermons before turning to her first love, writing romance fiction.

RITA award-winning author Anne McAllister writes fast, funny and emotional romances. You'll be hooked till the very last page!

Books by Anne McAllister

HARLEQUIN PRESENTS®

1620—CALL UP THE WIND
1680—CATCH ME IF YOU CAN
1769—THE ALEXAKIS BRIDE
1854—A BABY FOR CHRISTMAS
1890—FINN'S TWINS!
1932—FLETCHER'S BABY!
2005—THE PLAYBOY AND THE NANNY

Don't miss any of our special offers. Write to us at the following address for information on our newest releases.

Harlequin Reader Service
U.S.: 3010 Walden Ave., P.O. Box 1325, Buffalo, NY 14269
Canadian: P.O. Box 609, Fort Erie, Ont. L2A 5X3

ANNE McALLISTER

Gibson's Girl

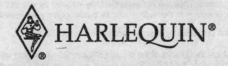

TORONTO • NEW YORK • LONDON
AMSTERDAM • PARIS • SYDNEY • HAMBURG
STOCKHOLM • ATHENS • TOKYO • MILAN • MADRID
PRAGUE • WARSAW • BUDAPEST • AUCKLAND

For Samantha Bell and Tessa Shapcott
—wise and supportive editors both—
Gib and Chloe (and I) thank you

ISBN 0-373-12060-5

GIBSON'S GIRL

First North American Publication 1999.

CHAPTER ONE

THERE were six naked women in Gibson Walker's line of sight. They were slender, lissome women with long legs, smooth thighs, and pert breasts.

And all he could think was, Why in hell weren't there *seven*?

He glanced at his watch, tapped his foot, ground his teeth.

"Where *is* she?" he muttered for the fiftieth time in the past half hour.

How was he supposed to shoot the photos for the brand-new fragrance *Seven!* if he only had *six* naked women?

"Can't we start?" one of the naked women whined.

"I'm cold," bleated another, hugging herself.

"I'm *hot*!" purred a third, batting her lashes at Gibson in an all too obvious attempt to make him hot, too.

But any temperature elevation in his body, Gibson knew, would have more to do with the heat of his growing irritability than with any woman's seductive wiggle. To make that fact clear he glared at her. She immediately edged behind a light reflector to avoid his gaze.

"Gibson, my nose is shiny," one of them complained now, studying herself in the mirror, tipping her head this way and that and making rabbit faces.

They won't be looking at your nose, sweetheart, Gibson wanted to tell her. But he knew better. This was Art—in the eyes of marketing, at least. So all he did was say to the makeup girl, "Judi, powder her nose."

Judi powdered the girl's nose. She powdered someone else's cheeks. Sierra, the hair stylist, fiddled for the thousandth time with everybody's hair.

Gibson tapped his toes, drummed his fingers, yelled at

Edith, the studio manager, to find out who the hell she was, this missing female.

Whose *fault* she was, he meant.

Given a choice Gib always picked his own models—ones he knew, ones he trusted to be reliable, professional, *on time*.

But he hadn't picked any of these. The client had.

"We want a little of everything," the ad rep had told him on the phone. "All beautiful, of course," he'd added hastily, "but not all...you know, standard brand."

Gibson had snorted at the time, but he knew what the rep meant.

Seven!, according to the ad-babble he'd been given, was supposed to appeal to Everywoman. Therefore Everywoman—albeit beautiful—was supposed to be in the ad. In other words, not cookie-cutter dark-haired, expressionless models with chiseled cheekbones and pouty lips.

"We'll look through the head sheets and pick them," the rep had promised. "Some tall, some short. Curly hair. Straight. A variety of ethnic types." Like it was somehow bold and daring. "And we'll send them over."

Fine with him. Gibson didn't care who was sent—as long as they could tell the time.

One of them obviously couldn't.

He drummed his fingers on the desktop. He paced. He fumed. The girls fumed, too. They fluttered. The fluttering grew. Agitation was next. Then, who knew?

Gibson, who counted on setting a mood for a shoot, could feel the mood of this one turning grim.

And then, all of a sudden, he heard Edith say, "Yes, yes. He's waiting for you. Go on right through. Go in."

The door opened. Slowly. Warily.

As well it might, Gibson thought.

"About time," he barked at the young woman who appeared in the doorway. "You were supposed to be here at one."

She blinked round eyes so deep and dark a blue they were almost violet. Gib shook his head. *The idiots in marketing strike again.* They knew he was shooting in black-and-white. The eyes were wasted.

"M-my plane was late."

"Plane?" They'd *flown* her in? Was she some hotshot West Coast model he'd never seen before? The latest L.A. superstar?

Gib's brows drew down, and he studied her more closely, trying to see whatever it was they'd seen in her. He was the one, after all, who was supposed to be a connoisseur of women.

It was what he did—photograph women. Beautiful women. It was what he was famous for—the photographs—and the ability to recognize beauty and capture it so others could see it, too.

He looked closely now.

Miss Blue-Violet looked like a caricature of the 1950s version of "the all-American girl." She was in her midtwenties age-wise, he'd guess. Older than the average "flavor of the month" they usually came up with. She wasn't especially tall, either. Average, he'd have said. Not average when it came to curves, though. He'd seen roads through Nebraska with more curves than the typical model. This one looked more like a real woman than that from what he guessed was camouflaged under her shirtwaist dress.

Who the hell wore a shirtwaist dress on a job like this? Who the hell wore a shirtwaist dress in New York City in this day and age? With her wavy blonde hair and full lips, she looked, for all the world, like a sort of discreet, demure, buttoned-down Marilyn Monroe.

And there was a contradiction in terms for you, he thought wryly.

Maybe that was what they saw in her—the potential to burst out, to become something more. Sprinkle on a little

Seven! and a woman could turn from the seven virtues to the seven sins.

Not a bad idea. A speculative smile touched Gibson's mouth. He could work with that.

"What's your name?" he asked her.

"Chloe," she said with a flutter of lashes designed to indicate bafflement, as if she thought he should have known.

Gibson's brows lifted. Was she going to be one of those arrogant ones, then? One of those models who'd done two or three jobs, maybe got a cover somewhere, and expected that she was now a household word? Gib had no use for prima donnas, even if their planes were late.

"Well, Chloe," he drawled, "you're here now, so take off your clothes and let's get this show on the road."

The blue-violet eyes seemed almost to bug out of her head. Her mouth opened, but no words came out. She only gaped at him. Her cheeks actually seemed to be turning red.

"What's the matter?" Gibson said, entirely unsympathetic. "Didn't the nice people tell you what you'd have to do if you came here today?"

"They didn't say…they didn't say…that." Chloe gulped. She looked around wildly, blinking as her gaze went from one naked woman to the next.

Generally models who'd been around a while were entirely unselfconscious, wandering around without a stitch on. Every one had seen so many naked people that they were too blasé to care. But now, under Chloe's stricken gaze, Gib could feel their self-consciousness rising. Next thing you knew they'd be grabbing for their robes.

Gib ground his teeth. Then he pasted a smile on his face. "Well, I guess you can leave," he said in saccharine tones. He leveled a challenging gaze at her. "I guess you can just get back on that plane and fly home again." He paused a beat. "Or you can do what you were hired for."

Dead silence. She seemed almost to stop breathing. Then she made a quick gasp. Her tongue touched her upper lip.

Gib could read indecision on her face. He almost thought he could read fleeting panic there, too.

Hell's bells, what had possessed them to hire this one?

And then, with one last desperate gulp, she nodded. "Wh-where do I...ch-change?"

"I'll show you." Sierra, the purple-haired stylist, smiled encouragingly at her and beckoned to her with long, be-ringed fingers. "This way."

With one last gulp and a sidelong glance in his direction, Chloe skittered after Sierra toward the row of changing rooms on the other side of the studio.

Gib could have sworn he heard her teeth chattering as she passed.

In the last twelve years, Gibson had photographed a lot of women.

His camera liked them. It traced their lines, their curves, their pouts, their smiles. It turned them into art. It made Gibson one of the most sought-after photographers in the business. From a professional standpoint he was pleased.

Personally he couldn't have cared less.

He didn't care about the women either. Gibson didn't get involved with the women he photographed.

He'd been there, done that. And he'd learned his lesson.

As far as he was concerned, they were nothing more than light and shadow, curve and angle, rise and fall.

It was the geometry of the lens and the body he concentrated on. Nothing personal. They might as well have been old tires or autumn leaves, these naked women. They were objects. They were interchangeable, all of them. Had been for years.

Until Chloe came out of the dressing room that afternoon.

Chloe wasn't just a curve or an angle, a light or a shadow. She was a person. Live. Breathing.

Trembling.

It drove him nuts.

"Okay. Let's go," he said, barely sparing her a glance, when she finally crept out of the changing room and slipped in behind the other models. "In a circle now. I need silhouettes. Arms over your heads. Reaching…that's right… reaching."

And seven women's arms went over their heads. Seven women reached, stretched.

Six moved smoothly, their gestures flowing, their bodies curving.

The seventh trembled.

Gib lowered the camera. "Chloe," he said. "Straighten up."

She gave him a quick desperate glance. She nodded. She ran her tongue over her lips. She straightened up.

"Reach," he commanded.

Chloe reached. Her hair bounced.

Her breasts did, too.

And Gib's mouth went dry. His palms went damp. His body got hard. Like he was some damn teenager, for heaven's sake!

He'd seen breasts before. Hundreds. Thousands. He'd probably seen more women's breasts in the last twelve years than most men did in a lifetime.

But most of the breasts he'd seen didn't—he ran his tongue over his lips—well, they didn't…bounce.

The other thousands of breasts Gib had seen had been firm, perky, plastic almost. And there had never been very much of them. Not even a handful.

Chloe was rather more…voluptuous.

The shirtwaist gone, she was Marilyn unbound.

Gib shut his eyes and shoved the thought away. But the moment he opened them, his gaze, and the thought, immediately snapped back right to her.

"Reach," he barked at her. And when she reached—and jiggled—he bit out, "I didn't say lunge, sweetheart! I said, reach. Like you're reaching for your lover."

Her whole body blushed.

Gibson lowered the camera. He blinked. He shifted position, disbelieving, wanting to see her more clearly. He'd never seen a full body blush. He was amazed. Intrigued. Enchanted.

Well, no. Not enchanted. That was stretching things *too* far.

Gibson Walker was not enchanted by women. He hadn't been enchanted by any woman since...

He squelched that thought.

"Stop shaking," he commanded her. "Or I'll have six lovely ladies and a blur."

"S-sorry." But she still shook. She didn't stop.

Gib shook his head, then picked up the camera again. He shot. He moved. He directed.

"Swim," he told them. "Languid, easy movements overhead. Like you're going through water."

They swam. Easy overhand strokes. They went up on tiptoe. They floated.

Chloe jiggled.

Gib ground his teeth.

He looked away, focused on another of the women. They moved and Chloe hove into view once more. He cleared his throat and tried to find a rhythm. "Let's see those lips. Purse those lips. Kisses. I want kisses."

And damned if Chloe didn't look straight at him, face aflame, body blushing, lips pursed!

Gib blew out a harsh exclamation of air. "Not *me*, sweetheart!" he said in a slightly strangled tone. "I want profiles. Kiss your lover. You do have a lover, don't you?"

Whoa. The flush was back—with a vengeance. Too bad the ad wasn't going to be in color. That was some rosy glow.

Gib let out a pent-up breath. He wiped suddenly damp palms on the sides of his jeans, then ran his tongue over his lips. *Focus, damn it,* he told himself.

He *was* focusing. That was the problem.

Don't focus on her!

He tried not to. He moved, he crouched. He willed himself to ignore the growing insistence in his body. He pointed the camera at all seven women. Unerringly it found Chloe.

He tried to remember all the ways he wanted them to move. His mind was a blank. Well, no, not really a blank. There were very definite curves on his mind. A very definite body.

A very sexy body.

A *real* body. Unlike the other six, Chloe seemed to respond to his direction with more than her muscles. She was unguarded, open. He said, "Lover," and she blushed. He said, "Kiss," and he saw longing on her face.

"Yes," he said. "That's it. Like that. More. Give me more, sweetheart."

They all looked at him.

"Er, sweethear*ts*," he corrected. He smiled at them all. He looked at Chloe.

She trembled. She blushed. Her breasts jiggled.

Then he heard a commotion in the outer office. A "You can't go in there!" followed by "Of course I can. I'm late!"

And the door burst open and Tasha, a top flight model he'd worked with lots of times, burst into the room.

"Ah, Gibson, I am zo zorry! Zee taxi! Zhe break down! Zee driver! He say I can't leave without pay! I say, No pay! You don't go where I mus' go! No pay! Then he grab me! An' I scream! I say, he kidnapping me! He say, I cheating him! Oh!" She shook a yard of flaming red hair. "Zhose police! Zhey never listen! You zhink zhey would listen to be-you-tif-ul girl, yes? No! Zhey listen to dumbest taxi driver!"

And while she delivered this entire monologue, Tasha was busily flinging off her clothes. First the skimpy halter top, then the minuscule bra. One foot came up and a sandal slipped off. The other followed. She unzipped her mini-skirt and wiggled it past mini-hips over mini-thighs down ski slope legs.

"I tell you, zhese police, zhey know from nozhing!" To punctuate her declaration, she peeled off her underpants and flung them in the air. Then she lifted her arms and beamed at Gibson.

"We begin now, yes? I am ready!"

In the silence that followed, Gibson was conscious of shutting his mouth.

He was conscious of looking from Tasha, standing bare and beautiful in the middle of the room, full-frontal fantastic and not jiggling at all, to the rest of the naked women who surrounded her.

His gaze moved slowly. From body to body to body. From face to face to face. They looked at him, then at each other. Their eyes seemed to be doing the same thing his were.

Counting.

One. Two. Three. Four. Five. Six.

His eyes went to Chloe. Trembling. Jiggling. Blushing. Seven.

And Tasha made...

Eight.

Eight?

"Wait a minute," Gibson said. "There's something wrong here. If Tasha's supposed to be here—"

"Of courze I'm zupposed to be here!"

But Gibson went right on. "Then somebody else is not."

And as one, they all turned to look at Chloe.

She slapped her arms across her breasts and ducked behind the table. Her face—*her whole body*—was as red as Tasha's hair. If he'd thought she was blushing before, it was nothing compared to this.

"You're not a model." Gibson's eyes narrowed. He glared at her accusingly.

"A model? Of course not!"

It was the last thing he expected her to say. If she wasn't supposed to be here, he figured she was at least trying to horn in, to make a name for herself, take advantage where she could. It had happened before.

He scowled now, unprepared for such a prompt denial. If she wasn't a model, what the hell was she doing here and why had she taken her clothes off?

"Who are you?"

"I told you." She sounded almost desperate now. "I'm Chloe. Chloe Madsen. Your sister sent me—"

"My *sister*? *Gina* sent you?"

Her head bobbed. Behind her hands, he noticed, her breasts bobbed, too. Gib shut his eyes.

When he opened them it was to see her grab one of the robes that had been casually tossed across the table, and drag it on. Then she folded her arms across her chest. "Yes," she said. "Gina sent me. To work for you. For the summer. To be your assistant."

"Assistant." Gib dropped the word like a lead balloon.

"Yes," Chloe said firmly. "She said you'd agreed. Didn't you?"

Oh, God. Gib gritted his teeth.

"Probably," he said through them.

"Just...probably?" Chloe looked doubtful.

Oh, all right. "I suppose I must have," he muttered.

But only because he agreed to whatever Gina asked him to do. He owed Gina. Their parents had died when Gib was thirteen and Gina was twenty. She'd practically raised him, had given up college to come back and make a home for the two of them. Later she'd seen that he was able to go to university. She'd supported and believed in him his whole life.

He could never say no to the few things she asked.

But sometimes, when he really would have liked to, he

let her know from the tone of his voice that he really didn't want to do it. She'd never pushed it on him.

Until now.

Fury rising—though whether he was mad at Gina or Chloe or himself he couldn't have said—he yelled at Chloe now. "If you're supposed to be my assistant, what were you doing taking off your damn clothes?"

"You told me to!"

It was that easy? Gib stared, stupefied. "You mean if I just walked up to you on the street and said, 'Take off your clothes, Chloe Madsen,' you'd do it?"

"Of course not!" Her face, he noted with some satisfaction, now turned an even deeper shade of red. "But," she added after a moment, "when Gina told me I could come she stressed that I had to what you told me, that I was obligated to do whatever was required." A pause. "Jobwise."

Their gazes met. Clashed.

But she didn't look away. Gib had to give her credit. Chloe Madsen was a tryer—and she didn't back down.

She was breathing so hard he could see her breasts heaving slightly behind the soft terry fabric. He had a memory flash of what they'd looked like bare.

As blonde as she was, Chloe Madsen didn't have a blonde's fair skin. Her breasts had been a warm honey color, the peaks a dusky rose. Now she was wrapped in the equivalent of a terry bath sheet. He preferred her naked.

He suspected he wouldn't get to see her naked again.

Just as well, he thought, still very aware of how the sight of her had affected him.

Definitely just as well.

"Why you use zat girl?" Tasha's eyes flicked from Gibson to Chloe and back accusingly. "You cannot use zat girl! I am ze *Zeven!* girl!" She slapped hands on hips and glared at him.

"Tasha…" Gib began to placate her.

She took his face between her hands and planted a kiss 'on his mouth. "You ztart over, yes? You forgive Tazha for being late, yes?"

"Yes," Gib said automatically, stepping out of her reach. His gaze flicked back to Chloe who hadn't moved an inch. She was still looking at him—and he was looking back at her, not making any move to shoot.

"Gibzon," Tasha said impatiently.

He jerked his gaze toward her. "Huh?"

She tapped her bare foot. "We zhoot now?"

"Uh, yeah. We zhoo-shoot now." At last Gibson managed to tear his eyes away from Chloe Madsen. "We shoot." He turned back to the camera. "All right, let's start again," he said to the other women. "We'll take it easy. You know what to do."

They started to move in the circle again, Tasha sliding into the formation easily, *not jiggling*, Gib was happy to note.

"What about me?" Chloe asked. "What should I do now?"

Gibson looked at her once more. His mind saw everything the white terry robe covered. His body tightened.

Fortunately so did his resolve.

"Go home."

Go home?
Go home?
She would never dare to show her face in Collierville, Iowa again!

Not after baring everything else in New York City!

Chloe huddled in the tiny dressing room and listened to Gibson Walker's gruff seductive baritone encouraging the models to reach and stretch and swim. Just the way he had encouraged Chloe to reach and stretch and swim.

Oh, God. She pressed her palms to her cheeks—the ones on her face!—and tried to stop them glowing. Fat chance.

Her whole body was glowing. Burning. From the inside out. If this was what hot flashes were like, she had no desire to hit menopause. Ever.

Not that she would.

She would surely die of embarrassment first.

She pulled on her underwear, then yanked her dress over her head, all the while breathing as if she'd just run a marathon. She could barely get the dress buttoned, her hands were shaking so badly. She stuffed her feet into her sandals, and thought she would never get the straps fastened. She didn't even try to refresh her gnawed-off lipstick. She was sure, if she did, she would look as if a demented three-year-old had colored all over her mouth.

So finally she was finished. Dressed. Armored.

And absolutely unable to leave the dressing room.

There was no way she was walking back out into that studio. No way on earth she was going to face the world— or Gibson Walker—again.

She was mortified.

And he'd been furious.

What did *he* have to be furious about?

She was the one who had taken off her clothes! He'd merely asked her to.

What had she been thinking?

Well, she hadn't, really. That much was obvious. If she had, she'd have realized that a photographer of Gibson Walker's stature had no interest at all in photographing a silly bumbling twit from Iowa, for goodness' sakes!

But at the time, with his demand ringing in her ears and the memory of his sister Gina telling her that Gibson might ask her to stand in for a model while he sets lights and things, well, she'd *misunderstood*! That was all.

Heck of a misunderstanding.

A tiny giggle escaped her.

It wasn't much of a giggle. The misery of it, the disgrace

and embarrassment of it were still too new and raw. But if she was honest, there was a funny side to it.

What on earth would Dave say?

Of course, he'd never know because Chloe was never, ever going to tell him! Dave Shelton, her fiancé, had enough misgivings about this summer job she had taken in the "big bad city." He still couldn't understand why she needed to go to New York at all.

"New York? You want to go to New York? What do you want to go out there and get corrupted for?" he'd asked more than once.

"It's a wonderful city. A fascinating city. There's so much to see and do. I just want to experience it. I'm not going to get corrupted," Chloe had assured him.

And she wasn't! But even so, he didn't need to hear how she'd paraded around naked in front of her employer!

No one was *ever* going to hear about that!

Unless—and here she gulped—unless Gibson Walker told them.

He wouldn't! Would he?

That thought zapped her with another flush, even hotter than the first. Oh, please, no! He couldn't!

"Kissing, ladies. Purse those lips," she heard him say.

She put her hands over her face, remembering how she'd looked straight at him and pursed hers. Merciful heavens! She truly might die.

And then, at last, he said, "Okay, that's it. Thanks a lot. I think we got some great stuff."

At once she heard the models begin chattering, the red-headed latecomer with the sexy accent—her replacement!—louder than all the rest. It was all "Gibzon thiz" and "Gibzon that." And Gibson answered, gruff but perfectly matter-of-fact, as if he worked with beautiful naked women every day of the week.

For all Chloe knew, he did!

There was the sound of shuffling bare feet as the models

came toward the dressing cubicles and doors opened. Someone rapped on her door.

"I'm...n-not ready," Chloe managed.

She would never be ready. If she could, she would stay in here the rest of her life.

Her fingers were trembling less. So she finished buttoning up her dress—closing it clear to the neck. Then she ran her palms down her sides, cinched the belt, and drew in a deep and—she hoped—steadying breath.

She tried to look sensible, demure, competent. She did look sensible, demure, competent—if you discounted the disarray of her wavy blonde hair and the hectic blush on her cheeks.

Yet scant moments before she had been anything but!

Beyond the door she could hear the other girls getting dressed. They laughed and chattered. The doors to the dressing rooms banged open.

"Bye, Gib!"

"See you soon!"

"Love you, Gib."

With a chorus of cheery goodbyes, they departed—until there remained only silence.

And Gibson Walker.

It was, Chloe knew, the moment of truth.

Some would say, Chloe was sure, that cavorting naked around a room was a moment of truth of sorts.

Perhaps it had been. After all, could whatever came next possibly be worse? As far as she could see, she had two options. She could sneak out, never show her face here again, and take the next plane back to Iowa, admitting defeat before she even got started. Or she could face the man on the other side of the door, swear that she would be a good assistant, and buckle down and live up to her word for the rest of the summer.

Put like that, there wasn't any choice.

Chloe wanted this summer. She *needed* this summer. She

had turned her own and Dave's lives upside down for this summer. It was on the order of a spiritual journey, she'd told him.

He hadn't understood. She supposed she couldn't really expect him to. But if she really believed what she'd told him, she couldn't go home.

Not now. Not yet.

Chloe took a deep breath, crossed her fingers, and opened the door.

"I've got you a plane reservation," he told her briskly the minute the door opened. "You leave at six, get into Chicago at nine. There's an hour layover. You'll get the last flight to Dubuque and be there by 11:15. You can call someone to pick you up."

He gave her one quick glance—and not only to see if she was wearing clothes and if her breasts still jiggled. Though he couldn't help noticing that she was and they weren't. Then he made himself concentrate on the pile of junk that had been accumulating on his desk for the past twelve years.

It seemed suddenly imperative that he sort through it.

When she didn't reply, he glanced up again, careful to keep his eyes firmly on her face. Unfortunately that was where her lips were. Damn.

She was looking at him with a worried, woebegone expression on her face.

"I'll pay for it," he said impatiently, because he was willing to bet she was worrying about the cost.

"It's…it's not that. It's…I can't go home."

"*What?*" Gib's brows snapped down. "What do you mean, you can't go home? Of course you can go home!"

But Chloe Madsen just shook her head adamantly. "No. I can't. Not until August 15th, anyway."

"They banished you from Iowa until August 15th?"

Granted, he hadn't been back to Iowa once in the past

dozen years, but it didn't seem likely they'd instituted quota laws that would prevent people from returning.

"I said I would be back August 15th," she said as if that were explanation enough.

It wasn't. "So? They got a phone? Call them and tell them you'll be back sooner. Call them now and tell them you'll be back tonight."

But she only shook her head. "I can't."

Gib felt a muscle in his jaw twitch. "Why the hell not?"

Chloe Madsen twisted her fingers. Her gaze flicked just a second in his direction. The blue-violet eyes blinked rapidly.

"Stop that!" Gib snapped.

Her eyes went wide. "Stop what?" She looked baffled.

"Crying. Don't you dare cry."

Her chin lifted. "I never cry."

Gibson snorted a reply. He wasn't going to argue about it.

"I don't," Chloe said firmly, taking his snort in exactly the vein in which it was intended. "Not about jobs, anyway," she qualified after a moment. She hesitated, then took a deep breath. It made her breasts lift—and settle.

Gib shut his eyes. He turned away, headed for the door, opened it and stood waiting for her to go.

Edith, his office manager, was still sitting at her desk. She looked up now with interest. Gib hoped her being there would encourage Chloe not to continue the discussion.

"I know I made a fool of myself this afternoon," Chloe said, her voice soft but firm. So much for his hopes. "But when we were talking about the job, Gina and I, I told her I was willing to do whatever an assistant did. And, well, one of the things she said they did was to stand in for models. I...wasn't thinking. I should have realized you weren't just setting up and running through. But I thought it was...expected of me. And then when you told me if I didn't want to do it, to get back on the plane and go home...well, I couldn't do that, either!"

"Why not?"

She looked at him as if he were crazy. "Because I couldn't! Not after I'd made such a fuss and—" She stopped, clamped her lips together, didn't say another word.

"Fuss?" Gib encouraged helpfully. What sort of fuss?

But she didn't respond. Eventually she said, "Look, it was an honest mistake. I feel like an idiot. I must have looked like an idiot."

No, she had looked...memorable. He didn't figure he would forget Chloe Madsen swimming naked around his office as long as he lived. He also didn't figure she wanted to hear that.

She bit her lip. "I really want to do this. Be your assistant, I mean. Please, don't hold what I...what I did...against me." She looked at him beseechingly.

"I don't hold it against you," he said roughly. "But you still can't stay."

"But you told Gina—"

"No," he corrected her, "Gina told me. Gina is always telling me what I need to do, and I just sort of let it go in one ear and out the other. I go uh-huh, uh-huh, uh-huh at appropriate intervals."

"Well, you obviously should have gone 'huh-uh' at one of them," Chloe said just a little tartly. It was the first bit of spirit he'd seen from her since she'd come out of the dressing room.

"I never thought she'd actually send you!"

"Well, she did. She assured me that you'd agreed. She said you would let me work for you for two months. It's not a big deal."

"It's a big deal!"

She looked astonished. "Why?"

The innocence of her query stopped him dead. "Be-cause...because..." Because he didn't want an assistant like her—an *innocent* from Iowa, for heaven's sake! New York was a rough place, a hard place. A person needed to be sophisticated to survive. Chloe would get eaten in a matter of minutes.

"It wouldn't work," was all he said.

"You don't think I can do it! You think I'm incompetent." Her eyes accused him.

Gib scowled. "I do not! I'm sure you're very competent—"

"I am."

"—and I'm sure you'd make a fine assistant—"

"I would."

"—but I don't *want* an assistant!"

"You need one," Edith said.

Both Gibson and Chloe snapped around to stare at the older woman sitting behind the reception desk. She gave Chloe a little nod and Gibson a benign smile.

"You need one," she repeated.

"I have…what's her name…?" He could never remember their names. They didn't last long enough for him to bother to learn them. "Frosty?"

"Misty," Edith said patiently. "And she's about as reliable as her name."

"Right. Misty." He tried to make her sound tough and competent. She was neither. Misty was the latest in a long line of what Gibson called his "girls." The young women who schlepped and carried, set up lights and reflectors, ran errands, loaded film and lugged power packs.

"Girls." Edith sniffed every time he used the term. "That is totally politically incorrect."

"So sue me," Gibson muttered.

They were lucky he even recognized them as members of the species. Misty and her forerunners—he was sure there had once been one called Frosty—came in all shapes and colors and sizes. They also invariably came with nose rings, spiked hair, black leggings and very little brain. They had the half-life of a loaf of bread. And were as memorable.

Gibson figured he'd remember Chloe for a good long while.

"We're going to need someone reliable," Edith reminded him, "because I'm going to Georgia's next week."

Gibson scowled. He didn't want to think about that. He relied on Edith for everything unconnected with the actual shooting of photos. She ran the studio, kept the ad reps at bay, dealt with the agencies, the caterer, the legion of bike messengers who rang the buzzer in the middle of his work. She was the person who kept him sane. He'd been appalled when she'd asked for a month off.

"A *month*?" She hadn't taken more than a week at a time in the last ten years.

"A month," she'd said firmly. "At least. I'll need it to help Georgia with the babies."

After fifteen years of a childless marriage, Edith's daughter, Georgia, had picked this summer to be inconsiderate enough to have triplets!

"Three?" Gibson had been aghast when Edith had told him. "What's the matter with just one?"

But apparently the quantity hadn't been up for discussion.

"We'll take all we can get," Edith had said cheerfully. She was over the moon about going to North Carolina and helping out with her first grandchildren. In fact she could hardly wait.

Gibson hadn't been able to say no. He knew she would have simply quit if he had. So he'd said, all right. But once he'd agreed, he'd shoved the thought right out of his mind.

"Get someone to take your place," he'd finally told her yesterday when she'd asked if he had someone in mind.

"I think Chloe will do fine," Edith said now.

"*What?*" Gibson practically shouted.

But Edith just smiled her I'm-going-to-be-a-grandmother-

and-all-is-right-with-the-world smile. "She looks sane and sensible and responsible. And if your sister trusts her..."

"My sister—"

"Is a good judge of character," Edith said firmly. "If he doesn't want you as his assistant, you can take over for me, all right?" she said to Chloe. Then she looked at Gibson. "Do you want her?"

A damned unfortunate choice of words.

Gibson felt his tongue tangling with his teeth. No, damn it, he didn't want her! Not in his studio every day. Not even in his reception room. And not just because his body had had an inconvenient reaction to her, either.

But he knew he was stuck. Gina proposed, Edith disposed. And he, heaven help him, was caught in the undertow.

But he wanted one thing understood. He turned on Chloe. "I won't be responsible for you!"

She looked at him, startled. "Of course not!"

He poked a finger under her nose and waggled it. "I won't fight your battles for you or protect your innocence or mollycoddle you in any way!"

"I never asked—"

His finger stabbed the air, making his point. "I just want it clear. If you stay, you're on your own!"

She stood her ground, drat her. She even looked mutinous. He thought she might bite his finger.

"Yes, certainly!" she agreed. As he turned away, she asked almost belligerently, "Is there anything else?"

He whirled back. "Yes! You'll damned well keep your clothes on!"

CHAPTER TWO

OF COURSE Gib had to find her a place to stay. Gina reminded him that he'd told her he would.

"I did *what*?" he yelped.

She had called late that evening just to "check on things"—to see how "darling Chloe" was, and to find out where he'd arranged for her to stay.

"You said you'd find her a sublet," Gina told him.

He was sure he had done no such thing. "I said I'd find her a sublet? *I* said that? In those words?"

"Well, if you're going to sound like a lawyer about it," Gina said huffily, "I suppose those weren't your precise words. When we discussed it, I asked if you could find her a place to stay, a sublet or something, and you said sure, you guessed."

"I never thought—" But he couldn't tell her that he had come to count on her not following through. He owed her. A lot. And she rarely actually asked for anything.

Just this. Just...

Chloe.

"Nothing yet."

"Nothing?" Gina sounded horrified.

"Yet, I said," Gib muttered, beleaguered. "I'll find something."

"You won't be sorry," Gina said, all traces of huffiness gone at once. "I'm sure it will work out really well for both of you. Chloe was so eager to come. And she's such a hard worker, Gib. There is nothing you could ask that Chloe wouldn't do to help out."

"You don't say," Gib replied drily, biting on the inside

of his cheek to keep from telling Gina exactly what Chloe had already done.

She would be shocked. Hell, when he thought about it— about who she was—*he* was shocked. But he wasn't going to mention it. Chloe Madsen, naked, was a memory he had no intention of sharing with anyone.

"She's quite a good photographer in her own right," Gina went on. "Oh, not in your class, dear. But she shoots wonderful photos for the *Gazette*."

The *Collierville Gazette* was the local weekly newspaper. Gina was the business manager of the paper, so that was clearly where she and Chloe had connected. The photos Gib remembered in the *Gazette's* pages were of local Pork Queens, fiftieth wedding anniversary celebrants, high-school football players who scored winning touchdowns and, for variety, artful "scenic" shots of acres and acres of corn and soybeans.

"And this inspired her to want to come to New York?"

"Not exactly." Gina paused. "It had something to do with a nun, I think."

"A *nun*!"

"For a story she wrote. Chloe, I mean. It sparked off something in her. She's been a little restless, trying to figure out what she should do..."

Dance naked? Gib thought, smiling.

"She taught kindergarten for three years before she came to work on the paper."

"*Kindergarten?*" He'd seen a kindergarten teacher *naked*!

Worse, at the memory, Gib could feel a stirring in his body even now. At least her being a kindergarten teacher explained the prim shirtwaist dress.

"She was wonderful with the children. She loved it, but she was a little restless there, too. She thought maybe it wasn't what she ought to do forever, so she came to the paper last year."

"And she still isn't satisfied?" Gib asked.

"Well, I don't know that she isn't satisfied. But she's lived in Iowa all her life. She wants to see what's beyond the horizon."

The more fool she, Gib thought.

"She won't be able to cope with this," he told Gina bluntly. "She's too naive. Too innocent."

"Well, she'll have you and—"

"She damned well *won't* have me! I'm not Mary Poppins, you know!"

"Of course not," Gina said quickly. "I don't expect that. Not...really. I was just hoping you'd be sort of...aware of her."

Oh, he was that.

"She's very eager to learn whatever you can teach her—"

Oh, cripes, don't say that!

"—and you always seem to need a new assistant..."

Had she been talking to Edith?

"She's exactly the sort of girl I wish you'd—" Abruptly, Gina stopped.

There was a long silence. A pregnant silence. A silence Gib was determined not to fill. One which he hoped Gina wouldn't fill, either. He knew what she'd say if she did.

The girl I wish you'd marry.

It was no secret that Gina wanted him to get married and come back to Iowa. That was what she'd always hoped for, ever since he'd taken a summer internship with noted celebrity photographer Camilo Volante a dozen years ago.

At the time Gina had wondered why he would do something like that. "Celebrity doesn't interest you," she'd said.

And Gib had replied, "But people do." It was people he wanted to photograph. Working for Camilo Volante had seemed like a terrific opportunity to learn from one of the world's foremost photographers of famous people. Then he could take it from there, using what he'd learned, photographing whoever he wanted.

That had been the plan, at least.

He'd expected then that he would go back to Iowa.

But life had a way of changing those plans. And the summer job had turned into an autumn one. And after that, well, things had changed. Irrevocably.

And Gib had never come back.

Now Gina appreciated that he was a success as a fast-lane, high-style photographer of beautiful women. But she still never hesitated to ask what had happened to his dream of shooting photos of people from all walks of life. And she also never hesitated to say how much nicer she thought it would be if he would find a lovely young woman, marry her, come back to Iowa and take photos of farmers—and Pork Queens.

Or maybe, just this once, she did hesitate.

"I'm not interested," Gib said firmly, in case she thought she had subliminally made her point.

"Interested? Oh, you mean…in Chloe?" Gina laughed lightly. "Of course not. And Chloe's not interested in you, either. She's only there for a break, Gib. Anyway she's engaged. She's getting married in September."

Married? Chloe?

Gib felt oddly breathless, as if someone had punched him. It was the most unexpected feeling he'd ever had. It puzzled him. Why should he care?

He *didn't* care.

It was just that all of a sudden his mind offered him a reprise of a very naked, very rosy, very jiggly Chloe Madsen—and she didn't look like anyone's fiancée!

"Who's the idiot letting her run around loose?" he demanded.

"If you're asking who she's engaged to, it's Dave Shelton. He's a very nice young man. You remember Ernie and Lavonne Shelton? They farm north of town. Dave is their son.''

Gib vaguely remembered the name. ''There was a Kathy Shelton,'' he said, ''in my class.''

''Dave's older sister. She got married and moved to Dubuque. Then about three years ago, she divorced and came home with her kids. Until a couple of months ago, she was living in a mobile home on the farm where Dave and Chloe had been going to live. She's the reason they didn't get married three years ago.''

''They've been engaged for three years?''

''Not three,'' Gina said. ''Eight, I think.''

''Eight!''

''I'm talking out of turn,'' Gina said quickly. ''I don't know all the particulars, so I shouldn't be gossiping.''

Gib was willing to bet Gina knew almost every particular. In a town the size of Collierville, everyone knew everyone else's particulars.

But Gina just said, ''I'll let you go now, darling. Just keep me posted. And if you want to know more about Chloe and Dave, I'm sure Chloe will be happy to tell you. Just ask her.''

The hell he would.

Chloe supposed she ought to be feeling guilty.

She knew Gibson Walker did not want her working for him. If he could have turned her out onto the street and slammed the door on her back, she thought he would have.

Sensing how he felt, she knew she ought to say, Fine, I'll leave.

But she didn't.

She'd made such a deal out of leaving home—of *needing* this two months away, just to say she'd been out in the big wide world once—that she couldn't just give up and go back home and tell Dave she'd changed her mind.

He would want to know why.

And Chloe, being Chloe and incapable of dissembling, would have had to tell him—about the mix-up, about the naked photo shoot, about what a fool she'd made of herself.

And there was no way she was going to do that.

So she was staying. And she only felt the tiniest bit guilty. There was no room for guilt in a soul so full of embarrassment.

Now, hours later, high up in the hotel room where Gibson had unceremoniously stashed her, she pressed her face to the glass and saw, not the Empire State Building out her window, but her own silly self prancing around in the buff—and she still wanted to die.

But not yet, she admitted.

First she wanted her two months in New York.

The phone rang.

She picked it up. "Hi," she said, knowing it had to be Dave. She'd called him as soon as she'd come upstairs, forgetting the time difference and that he would be out doing the milking for at least another hour. She'd left him a message with a number to call her back.

"Hi yourself. Are you fulfilled yet?"

She almost smiled. "Not quite yet. How are you?"

He was fine. Of course he would be. She'd only seen him sixteen hours ago. But he told her anyway. He told her about his day, about the weather, about the cows, about the meal he'd just had with his parents at their house.

"Mom invited me for supper. I think they wanted to see if I'd show up alone, if you were really gone," he told her. "They can't believe you're really doing this."

Most people couldn't.

The twelve hundred and forty-two people who called Collierville, Iowa home were not given to eagerness when it came to spending a summer in New York City. Everyone she'd told thought she was out of her mind.

Chloe had given up trying to explain—except to Dave.

She needed Dave to understand. She'd thought he would.

She and Dave had grown up together. They'd played as children. They'd gone steady in high school. They were serious about each other when everyone else was still playing the field.

Chloe had always assumed she and Dave were destined for each other. Certainly there was nothing about Dave she didn't know.

And nothing he didn't know about her—except that she'd danced naked this afternoon!

"You're happy?" he asked her now.

"So far," she said. There was room for a tiny bit of happiness along with the embarrassment. So it wasn't a lie.

"Is it all you were expecting?"

"More, actually." And wasn't that the truth!

Fortunately he didn't ask what she meant. "So where are you staying? What's it like?"

She told him about the hotel. It was a no-frills place. "Respectable," Gib had told her. "Safe." She remembered a muscle in his jaw ticking as he'd steered her in. "Wish they had locks on the outside of the doors, too," he'd muttered.

She wasn't sure what he meant by that. She hadn't asked.

Dave was surprised. "I thought you were going to rent somebody's apartment."

"This is just temporary. He hasn't found a place yet." She didn't tell Dave he'd been hoping against hope that she wasn't coming.

"You're not staying with him!"

"Of course not!"

Gibson Walker didn't want her at his apartment any more than Dave wanted her there. There had never been any question. When he'd realized he was stuck with her, he'd taken her to this hotel.

"I can't afford a hotel," she'd protested.

"I can," he'd said in a voice that brooked no argument.

He'd marched her up to the desk and paid for one night's lodging.

She'd dug into her purse for her credit card. "I can manage one night!"

But he hadn't paid any attention. He'd checked her in, handed her bags to the bellboy, tipped him, told her he hoped she came to her senses by tomorrow and went home. And then he'd turned on his heel and started toward the door.

"Wait!" Chloe had called, and he'd stopped, then turned. "What time do we start in the morning?"

For a long moment he'd just looked at her. Then a corner of his mouth had twisted and he'd replied. "First shoot's at nine." Then he'd turned again and strode out the door.

"I'll find a place tomorrow," she told Dave now. "After work."

"A safe place," Dave instructed her.

"A safe place," Chloe agreed.

"I miss you."

"I miss you, too. But I'll be home before you know it."

"I'll know it," Dave said gruffly. "It's sixty-one more days."

He'd counted, Chloe realized guiltily. Well, so had she, but with anticipation, not annoyance.

"Compared to forever, sixty-one days isn't so long," she said gently. "And once I get home, we'll have forever."

And that was the truth. She had had Dave in her life for so long she couldn't imagine him not being there. Sometimes she wondered if she existed without him. Maybe that was what she was trying to find out.

"Sister Carmela has a lot to answer for," he grumbled.

"It wasn't just Sister Carmela."

But Dave wasn't convinced.

And he was right that it had been Sister Carmela, the new abbess at the monastery just outside Collierville, who had put the idea into Chloe's head.

She'd interviewed Sister last month for the newspaper. They'd hit it off at once, going on to talk much longer than the actual interview required. And in the course of their conversation, Sister Carmela had told Chloe not just about her new position as abbess, but the spiritual journey that had brought her there.

She had, she'd told Chloe, come to the abbey just after college, fresh with the enthusiasm and idealism of youth.

"I loved it," she'd said, her brown eyes sparkling. "I felt at home at once. More alive. Centered. As if this was where I'd always been meant to be. And everything went smoothly until right before I was to make my final profession. And then I began to get worried. What if I was wrong? What if I was foreclosing on my options too soon? What if I was doing this just because it seemed easy for me? Maybe too easy? I got restless, fidgety, unsettled."

Chloe, who had been feeling some of those very same feelings for the past few months, leaned forward earnestly and held her pencil, poised to note the reply. "How did you overcome it?"

"I didn't," the abbess told her with a smile. "I left."

"Left?" Chloe dropped the pencil. Scrabbling to pick it up, she'd looked up at the nun again to see if she was joking.

But though there was a smile on Sister Carmela's face, she was apparently quite serious. "I couldn't stay. Not until I was sure. So I decided to test my vocation, to go out, live in the 'real world' for a while and see if that was where I belonged. So I did."

Chloe smiled. "And that's when you realized...you didn't like it?"

Sister Carmela shook her head. "I did like it. A lot. It was wonderful, and by the 'real world's' standards, I was a success. But in the end, I knew it wasn't right for me. I saw that, no matter how 'successful' I was out there, I belonged here. And so I came back."

It made sense. It made an incredible amount of sense.

While Sister Carmela had been talking about her monastic life, she might as well have been talking about Chloe's.

She'd been feeling every bit as unsure, every bit as restless as the date she and Dave had finally set for their wedding approached. Granted it had been, at that time, still four months off. But some nights Chloe couldn't sleep. She kept thinking about the rest of her life...and wondering if it was going to be any different than what she'd already had.

It wasn't that she was dissatisfied really. It was just that *she didn't know!*

She and Dave had been together so long, they seemed so perfect for each other—like Sister Carmela and the monastery—that it made her nervous.

"You're asking for trouble," Dave said.

But Chloe knew that wasn't true. She was asking for a test. She needed to see what was beyond the rolling hills and river bluffs of the northeastern Iowa town where she'd grown up. Collierville was wonderful. Dave was wonderful. She loved them both. But maybe, like Sister Carmela, she was taking the easy way out.

Maybe she should leave, too.

"Not for fifteen years!" Dave had said when she told him how long Sister Carmela had stayed away.

"Of course not! A couple of months. That's all. What do you think?"

"I think it's nuts," Dave had said with his customary bluntness. "What's out there that isn't here? Besides crime, poverty, dirt and air pollution, that is."

Dave knew they had all that, to some degree, in Iowa. He was just trotting out the time-honored arguments that all self-satisfied midwesterners indulged in when they felt morally superior to big city folks.

But in the end, he'd supported her. He'd told his parents that if Chloe felt she had to do it, then she had to do it. He'd told her parents that he didn't mind waiting to get married. They'd waited often enough.

"I'll be back in August," Chloe had reminded them all.

"Leaving me to do all the work," her mother had said darkly.

But in fact, Chloe thought her mother was secretly pleased. She had far more interest in making it a wedding to remember than Chloe did.

"I'll take the phone book with me. I'll contact the florist, the caterer," Chloe promised. "I'll send out the wedding invitations from there."

She'd brought the phone book. But she wasn't working on lists of florists and caterers tonight. Tonight she was staring out at the New York skyline, periodically pinching herself, hardly able still to believe she was here.

It was going to be wonderful. The experience. The job. She would do a good job—she was determined about that. Despite her disastrous, humiliating beginning, she would salvage her job. And she would go home at peace, having seen the bright lights and big city; she would be ready to settle down with Dave.

Like Sister Carmela, she would get her taste of the big broad world, and then she would go home.

"The grass isn't greener on this side of the fence," she said aloud now. Then she giggled. From where she stood and looked out the window, there wasn't any grass to be seen at all.

She closed her eyes and thought about Iowa. She thought about how green the grass was now, how blue the sky. She thought about Dave. Strong. Steady. Dependable. Dave.

He was all she'd ever wanted in a man.

But just before she went to sleep she found herself hoping that, when she came to him naked on their wedding night, he would look at her with the same intensity that Gibson Walker had.

You'd think Gina had an in with the Almighty!

Well, Gib admitted, maybe she did. She was always doing

good deeds and helping other people. Maybe that was why everything she wanted for Chloe seemed to be falling into place.

He'd just been standing there by Edith's desk, telling her that if she wanted to keep Chloe she'd have to find her a place to stay, when the door opened and Sierra, the hair stylist, came in.

"She's staying?" Sierra sounded delighted. "Your sister's friend? You're kidding."

"I wish I was," Gib grumbled. "She won't leave."

Sierra's eyes got big. "Took one look at you, did she? Decided she can't live without you?" Sierra came in to do hair frequently on Gib's shoots. She knew how many women flung themselves at his feet. She also knew it irritated the hell out of him.

"She's engaged," Gib said dampeningly.

Sierra blinked in surprise. Then she shrugged. "You could cut him out."

"*I'm* not interested!"

The force of his voice had Sierra stepping backwards. She lifted her shoulders again. "You never are, are you?" It was common knowledge that for all that women threw themselves at Gib, he never chased them. He dated, but never seriously.

"No," he said firmly now. "I'm not."

"So," Sierra changed the subject, "when's she coming in?"

Gib shrugged. "I told her we started at nine. So we'll see if she actually shows up. Maybe by today she's come to her senses. Maybe," he said hopefully, "she got to thinking about it and went home this morning."

The door opened. "Who? Me?" Chloe said.

Gib groaned. Partly because she was still there—and partly because she looked every bit as sweet and innocent and delectable as she had the day before. He'd told himself he was imagining it.

He hadn't been.

She also looked fresh and bright and well-rested—a whole lot better rested than he was. And though her cheeks were rosy, if it was from mortification over yesterday's disaster, she didn't look nearly as mortified as he might have hoped.

Actually the blush on her cheeks looked more like brimming good health than lingering embarrassment. She looked like she could hardly wait to get to work.

"I haven't found you a place to stay," he told her flatly.

"My sister needs a house sitter," Sierra said.

Both Gib and Chloe jerked around to stare at her.

Sierra shrugged. "If you need a place to stay," she said to Chloe, "you can probably stay at my sister's. She's having her apartment redecorated this summer. They're doing a lot of work on it and she's going out to the Hamptons while they're working, but she was saying just the other day that she'd like someone to keep an eye on things, be there when the plasterers showed up, that sort of thing."

Chloe's eyes lit up. "Fantastic."

"Hang on a minute," Gib objected.

They all looked at him. He opened his mouth again, then closed it. What was he going to say? That he didn't think that the apartment of the sister of a purple-haired stylist was appropriate lodging for a former Iowa kindergarten teacher no more worldly than her students?

"She doesn't look like me," Sierra said with a grin, as if she could read his mind. "Mariah is...normal."

"I didn't mean that," Gib began, then stopped. What did he care? As he'd been at pains to point out to both Gina and Chloe, he wasn't going to be anyone's keeper. He shrugged irritably. "Fine. Ask your sister." He jammed his hands into the pockets of his jeans, then turned away. "Save me the trouble. I've got work to do," he said and stalked off toward the studio.

Footsteps hurried after him. "Wait for me," Chloe said a little breathlessly.

But Gib didn't want Chloe underfoot right now. He was entirely too aware of her at the moment. "Go help Edith," he said. "When Misty gets here she can help me."

He glanced long enough to see a flicker of disappointment on her face. His jaw tightened. He steeled himself against it. Telling her to help Edith was not the same as kicking a puppy, damn it.

The door to the outer office opened again, and the first models came in chattering. "Hi, Gib!"

"Hi, handsome!"

Gib flashed them standard smiles, then turned a scowl on Chloe again. "Go," he said. "Didn't you agree to do whatever I asked you to do?" he reminded her silkily.

She colored slightly. She sighed. She went.

Gib turned back to load film in the camera. Sierra started to work on the blonde model's hair. Beyond the door he could hear Edith telling Chloe about how she arranged the scheduling.

"Let me make some notes," Chloe said.

Gib nodded, satisfied. If she had to be here, helping Edith was the best place for her. She could have her time in the city, and she wouldn't be underfoot.

Now, if Misty would just show up.

He needed her to set up the lights and the reflectors so they could get started as soon as Sierra finished with the models' hair. He would need her to move things later, changing the lighting while he shot.

He read over the notes the agency had sent. He made some of his own. He started setting things up himself, annoyed.

Edith stuck her head in. "Misty called. She can't come in today. Something about her planets not being properly aligned."

Gib stared.

Edith shrugged, a small smile playing around the corner of her mouth. "Apparently she's sensitive to that sort of thing."

Gib gave her a steely-eyed glare.

"Shame about that," Edith said, still smiling. "You could probably use some help."

Gib could see Chloe sitting at Edith's desk, talking on the phone to someone, taking notes studiously, her lower lip caught between her teeth. Gib looked at her, then at Edith.

Edith looked at Gib, then at Chloe, then back at Gib.

Damn it, was she going to make him beg?

"I could send Chloe in to help when she's finished on the phone," Edith ventured after a moment.

"Do that," Gib growled.

Chloe came in five minutes later. "What can I do?" she said eagerly.

"Set these up." Gib pointed to the reflectors. He indicated where. Chloe went to work.

Gib was used to Misty and her predecessors—girls who needed to be directed and prodded every step of the way. Chloe didn't. Once he told her what to do, she did it. And the next time he needed it done, she did it without his having to say a word. She seemed almost to anticipate his directions. And she didn't say a word, either. Just worked.

He was amazed.

Chloe took it all in her stride.

And when they'd finished and the models had left, only then did she look at him and beam. "That was fun!"

Misty had never called it fun.

"Yeah," Gib said gruffly. "Here." He thrust the camera at her. "Can you load this?"

Solemnly, almost reverentially in fact, Chloe took it from him. While he watched, she loaded film into the camera. "That's another of your jobs," he told her.

Just as she was handing it back, Sierra came in. "I called

my sister. She'd like Chloe to come over this evening at seven.''

"We'll be there," Gib said.

Both Chloe and Sierra looked at him, then blinked.

He scowled. "Gina would want me to make sure it's the right place for her," he said. "Don't stare at me like that. She's my sister. She doesn't ask for much!"

"Right." Sierra nodded wisely.

Chloe gave him a bright, entirely unnecessary smile. "Thank you."

"Don't thank me," Gib said. "Let's get to work."

Naturally Chloe thought Mariah's apartment was wonderful.

A day in Chloe's company had shown Gibson the truth of everything he'd feared: she thought the city was wonderful. Period.

"It's just so…so…alive," she'd said on the way uptown in the taxi. "Look!" She'd pointed at a man in top hat and tails, playing a grand piano on a street corner. "Wherever you look, you never know what you'll find!"

"That's not necessarily good," Gib had said gruffly.

But Chloe hadn't stopped enthusing. She enthused about the neighborhood in which Mariah lived. It was on the Upper West Side, not too many blocks above and just a little west of Gib's own apartment on Central Park West. Not a bad neighborhood at all, he conceded. But not exactly Iowa.

Still, he reserved judgement, going only so far as to say, "I'm the one who's deciding if it's all right or not. If it's not, you're not staying," just as they were alighting from the taxi.

"What?" Chloe looked astonished.

He took her suitcases and pointed her toward the brownstone whose address Sierra had given them. "You heard me."

Sierra's sister, Mariah, was normal. Attractive even, in a slender, long-haired, model-like way. Her hair was brown hair, not purple. Her fingernails were red, not black. And other than tiny studs in her ears, she had no visible body piercings.

Not that Sierra had any, either. But Gib suspected she had leanings in that direction.

Mariah ushered them in and up the stairs. "I'm on the second floor. A floor-through. Everything has been pretty much gutted since I bought it this spring. The building was a wreck when I bought my place. Plaster crumbling. Wallpaper peeling. Ceilings sagging. But it's down to the bare bones now, and the plasterers are supposed to be starting later this week."

The apartment faced south. It was, as Mariah claimed, almost cavern-like. She had no furniture in the living room besides a television and VCR and a futon with a brightly colored Indian coverlet and lots of pillows. The kitchen was equally spartan. Appliances, a bar stool and a butcher block stacked with a small assortment of pots and pans and dishes.

"The stove is gas," Mariah said. "It works. The water runs. Hot and cold. The refrigerator is hooked up. There's a light overhead." She gestured at the shop light hanging from the ceiling fixture. "Once they've plastered in here, the cabinet maker will begin working. Then they're going to bring in the counter tops. They might have to shut things off briefly, but for the most part, you shouldn't have any problems."

Chloe took it all in wordlessly. Gib had a hundred questions.

Were these workers licensed? Bonded? Responsible? Did they have criminal records?

"Next thing you'll be wanting to see their high school transcripts," Chloe said irritably.

"You can't be too careful," Gib told her.

"I'm sure they're very reliable," Mariah said. She led

the way into the bedroom at the back of the apartment. It needed plastering, too. But there was a queen-size bed and another pile of colorful pillows in the center of the room. It looked too big for one person, Gib thought nervously. Would some man talk her into bringing him home to share it? Would her farmer fiancé fly out for weekend trysts?

What difference did it make?

"The plasterers and cabinet maker all worked on the apartment downstairs," Mariah went on. "It was finished this spring and it's wonderful. I'll ask Rhys to show you," she said to Chloe.

"Rhys? Who's that?" Gib wanted to know.

"My neighbor," Mariah said. She pointed downstairs. "We bought into the building at the same time. He's done a great job with his place. He has the bottom two floors. Seems a waste when he's single and hardly home enough to enjoy it." She shook her head. "He's a fireman. Goes all over the world putting out blazes. Oil wells, natural disasters, things like that."

Gib watched Chloe's eyes get bigger and bigger. He wished Mariah would confine herself to the relevant details.

"What days do they pick up trash?" he asked. "What about recyclables? Is someone checking that all this plastering gets done? Chloe won't be responsible for it."

"I've made a list." Mariah gestured toward some papers on the butcher block. "I've got it all written down, when everything is supposed to happen. It's not a big deal."

Gib snorted. Easy for her to say. She was going to be in the Hamptons. It would be Chloe who would be here. What if they were all axe murderers and rapists?

Well, he could hardly ask that. Not in so many words.

Chloe apparently had none of the same qualms. She picked up the list and smiled beatifically at Mariah. "No problem. Sounds like fun. And—" she looked at Gib, eyes shining "—I'll get to have a real New York experience."

Mariah chuckled. "That's for sure."

"She has a job," Gib reminded them. "She can't be here all the time."

"Oh, she won't have to be. Rhys can let them in."

"I thought he was all over the world. Never home long enough to enjoy it, didn't you say?" And now he was going to let people into the apartment. He had a key?

Mariah waved her hands. "Oh, you know how it is. When he's gone, he's anywhere. When he's home, he's downstairs. He'll be home for the next six weeks. I'm sure you'll meet him in the next few days," she said to Chloe, and confided, "He's a hunk."

Gib's teeth came together. "She's engaged," he said through them.

Mariah's eager smile faded for a moment, then brightened again. "Well," she said cheerfully to Chloe, "no harm in looking, is there?"

They shared a conspiratorial giggle. Gib drummed his fingers on the butcher block. When Chloe looked his way, he gave her a black scowl. She frowned right back at him.

What was that for? he wondered. He was only protecting the rights of her fiancé.

"I'm not sure he should have a key," Gib began.

But Chloe cut in. "I think this is very nice of you," she said to Mariah, just as if he weren't there at all. "And I'll be happy to let plasterers in or cabinet makers or whoever. I'm sure I'll be very happy here."

"I'm sure, too," Mariah said, ignoring him as well. "And I'll feel much better knowing that someone is living here."

They shook hands, all smiles. Gib glowered at them.

Then Chloe turned to him. "Well," she said briskly, "thanks for bringing me up here. It was very kind of you. I don't want to take anymore of your time, though. I know you're busy."

And she stood looking at him as if she wanted him to leave!

For a longer moment than Gib would have liked to admit, he didn't move. She was *dismissing* him?

Like hell. "As a matter of fact, I am busy," he said and glanced at his watch. "Got a date. Don't want to keep her waiting."

Then he gave her his best male-on-the-prowl look and headed for the door. At the doorway, he stopped and turned back. "You'll be there at nine tomorrow morning," he instructed her.

She blinked. "Of course."

He turned the handle. Then stopped again. "You can take the number nine train downtown. Get on at 79th, get off at 18th."

"All right."

He opened the door. Stopped again. "You know how to use the subway, don't you?"

"Of course." But he saw her swallow nervously before she pasted on a smile.

"I'll meet you," he said. "Just this once. Be at the station at 8:30."

"I'll show her the ropes," Mariah said cheerfully. "Don't worry about it," she told Gibson. "You just go on to work. She'll be there."

"That's right," Chloe said. "Mariah will show me." Then both of them stood there smiling at him, a united front.

Still Gibson didn't move.

"Your date?" Chloe said helpfully when the silence stretched on and on.

Gibson let out a harsh breath of air. "What?" Then, "Oh, right." He went out the door, hesitated a second longer, then shook his head and continued toward the stairs. He heard the door shut behind him and paused on the landing.

Was this what mothers felt like when they left their children on their first day of school?

CHAPTER THREE

CHLOE went to the subway stop with Mariah in the morning. She bought a packet of tokens as Mariah instructed her to do. She put her token in the slot and went through the turnstile.

"Very good," Mariah said from where she stood on the other side of the barrier. "You'll be a New Yorker in no time. Pretty soon this will all be second nature." She hesitated as the rush of commuting workers surged around Chloe. "Do you want me to come with you?"

Chloe shook her head no and gave Mariah a bright smile. "I'll be fine."

She felt happy, expansive, eager—the way she remembered feeling on her first day of school. She'd never been scared the way some children had been. On the contrary, for Chloe it had been the start of a big adventure.

So was this, she thought as she grabbed the overhead bar and hung on as the subway train rattled away—living in Manhattan, walking briskly along Broadway, taking the subway, jostled and bumped along with thousands of others on their way to work just as she was.

Working for Gibson Walker.

That was going to be the biggest adventure of all.

She wished she had asked Gina more about her brother. When Gina had proposed that Chloe go to work for him, all she could think about was New York, the big city, the challenges, the opportunities.

She hadn't given Gibson a thought.

She barely remembered him from her school days. He had been in high school when she'd been in the elementary grades. In a bigger town she wouldn't even have known who he was. But she remembered her older sisters, Kate and Julie, giggling about the handsome boys—and one of them had been Gibson Walker.

In fact when Kate had heard she was going to work for him, she'd said, "You lucky dog! He was always such a hunk. And the best thing was he didn't even know it."

Well, Chloe could have told her, he knew it now.

Not that Gibson was arrogant, really. Or not very, anyway. But he certainly knew women liked him.

How could he not with some of the world's most beautiful falling all over him every day?

But he knew how to handle it—knew how to handle *them*. Chloe had watched yesterday as he'd teased and cajoled the models who came in. He made the querulous ones laugh and the uptight ones relax.

He had an easy way with them, never taking them too seriously. He almost seemed indifferent at times. Yet they all seemed to adore him. They fluttered around Gibson like bees around a flower.

Was one of them the woman he'd had a date with last night? Chloe wondered. Which one?

She should have asked Kate and Julie what sort of girls he'd liked in high school.

Not that it made any difference, she told herself sharply. Gibson Walker's love life was of no interest to her. No interest at all!

It was of so little interest that, in telling herself not to think about it anymore, she almost forgot to get off at 18th Street.

She had to practically shout, "Excuse me! Sorry! I need to get off!" in order to push her way to the door and out onto the platform before the train rumbled away again.

"It isn't second nature yet, sweetie," she muttered to herself. "So don't start pretending you know what you're doing until you really know. Pay attention."

No one even looked at her as she talked to herself.

Yes, she was in New York.

It seemed to Gib there were three Chloe Madsens. At least.

There was the kindergartner Chloe.

She was the one who stared wide-eyed at skyscrapers and bumped into things because she was too busy gawking to pay attention to where she was going—the one who had accompanied him uptown last evening, for example, the one he was afraid to let loose in the big, bad city.

But then there was the businesslike, professional Chloe.

She was the first assistant he'd ever had who actually seemed able to "assist" him. Once he showed her what to do, she did it. And he didn't have to keep showing her—or even telling her. She anticipated his needs.

And every day this week she had actually shown up on time. All her planets were, unlike Misty's, apparently aligned, and she must have built in "gawk-time" for the kindergartner Chloe. She was, just as Gina had promised, a gem in the studio.

And there was the naked Chloe.

And *that* Chloe—the sensual, womanly Chloe in the altogether, whom he had not seen since that first afternoon—he couldn't seem to get out of his mind.

He should have been able to.

God knew he had seen far more of the kindergartner and the businesswoman over the past few days. In fact he'd barely caught a glimpse of any of the naked Chloe's rosy skin—other than her face, her neck, her forearms and her hands—since that first time.

Every day when she came to work she was always very discreetly dressed in casual linen trousers and neat, tailored shirts or gauzy belted shirts.

But he remembered.

Oh, Lord, did he remember!

He *knew* what was beneath those neat, tailored clothes

Chloe wore. And for all that she seemed to be contriving to be a sexless wonder this week—it didn't do any good.

It got so he actually found he was standing up when she sat down, hoping to get a glimpse down the open neck of her shirt! And when she actually caught him peeking one day, he scowled and grumbled and told her to keep her shirt buttoned if she didn't want to invite people to look at her.

And damned if, after that, she didn't!

What was he supposed to say then? *I didn't mean it? Unbutton your shirt? It's driving me crazy?*

He didn't say a word. She stayed buttoned up.

And that night he dreamed about her naked again!

Fortunately the next day was going to be her last in the studio because it was going to be Edith's last on the desk. She'd been spending every lunch hour with Edith learning the desk-side of the job.

She caught on quickly, Edith told him. "She'll do a great job, if you're sure you don't need her in the studio."

Chloe in the studio was the last thing Gibson needed.

After the dream he'd had the night before, he'd have been more than willing to send her back to Iowa, but he was very sure she wouldn't go—and equally sure that he would have to do some pretty heavy duty explaining to Gina if he tried to get his sister to persuade her to return.

No, it would be enough that she was out of the studio.

At least it would have been if he hadn't walked through late that afternoon when Edith had already left, and Chloe was there talking to Sierra about Rhys.

"Mariah introduced me last time I was there," Sierra was saying. "I couldn't keep from drooling. Isn't he just gorgeous?"

Gib waited for Chloe to say he was passable, but nowhere near as handsome as her fiancé, whose name he heard a hundred times a day at least.

But Chloe smiled sappily and said, "He is. And he's really nice. He came up last night and helped me move some of the furniture so the plasterers could get in the back bedroom.''

"Nice is good, but gorgeous is better," Sierra said.

Chloe laughed. "Best is both."

"I thought you were engaged," Gib said abruptly.

The two of them looked up at him, startled.

"Doesn't What's-His-Name mind when you ogle other men?" he continued.

He knew perfectly well what What's-His-Name's name was. Every other word out of Chloe's mouth was "Dave."

But now she only laughed and said, "I'm engaged, but I'm not dead, Gib. I can still appreciate a handsome man. After all, I appreciate you."

The moment the words were out of her mouth, she went fiery red—as if she'd never meant to say any such thing and had completely shocked herself.

Well, she'd shocked him, too! And damned if his own face didn't feel oddly warm. He couldn't remember the last time a woman had made him blush. Well, actually he could—and it didn't bear thinking about.

"Purely professionally, I mean," Chloe mumbled, averting her gaze and shaking her head.

Something about seeing her so clearly flustered made his own awkwardness fade. Gib grinned at her and winked. "Like I've appreciated you professionally, too," he drawled.

Sierra laughed.

Chloe's blush grew even more pronounced. "Go away," she told him, making shooing motions with her hands. "I've got phone calls to return."

"You're talking to Sierra," he pointed out.

"About work."

"About a hunk."

She shot him a steely look, then pressed her lips into a tight line. Then she stared straight ahead and drummed her fingers on the desk. She didn't look at him again. She did look as though her tightly buttoned collar was strangling her.

Gib bent toward her and touched the collar lightly. "Undo the button, Chloe," he said softly.

Her head jerked up. She looked at him, askance.

He shrugged negligently. "It doesn't cover anything I haven't already seen."

Despite Gib's reminders and occasional teasing comments, Chloe was pleased with her first week. She was getting her bearings.

She could do the subways, the buses, the taxis, if not like a native, at least with reasonable ease. And she had no trouble whatsoever doing her job.

The job was actually far more fun than she'd thought it would be. She'd expected she would be nothing more than a glorified gofer, but Gib actually let her take some of the instant photos before he began each shoot so he could check the lighting, study the shadows. When she hesitantly asked questions about why she was doing these things, he seemed very willing to explain.

And once he saw she was really interested, he always talked about what he was looking for, what he wanted to see, apparently believing he ought to teach her something if she was willing to learn.

She was very willing to learn.

Once, when he gave what amounted to a three hundred percent explanation to a small topic, he grinned and said, "If I'm boring you, tell me to shut up."

And Chloe, who could have happily listened to him for hours, replied, "You're not boring me." She'd almost said, I'd love to learn anything you want to teach me.

Fortunately she had the presence of mind *not* to say that!

She had heard too many of Gib's teasing remarks about her naked dance around his studio to ever leave herself open for the rejoinders that would doubtless come with a statement like that.

But as far as photography went, she was eager to learn from him. She had always liked taking photos of people more than of anything else. And watching Gib do it gave her the chance to learn from a master. She never would have thought that her feature photos would have anything in common with the high-gloss high-style commercial shots he took.

There could be nothing more artificial than the environment in which he worked, yet he did it easily, putting the models at ease and bringing out the best in each of them.

But when she'd said something about that, he'd just shrugged and replied, "People are the same."

And the longer she worked with him, the more she saw that it was true.

Heavens, he'd even got *her* to strip off and model—when she hadn't known better!

Not that he'd jollied her into it the way he cajoled and chatted with so many of the women he worked with every day.

She tried not to think about that day. She had plenty of other things to think about.

She found herself borrowing folders of Gibson's old tear sheets and photos, spending the evenings studying them, trying to learn from them, to see the way he saw.

He had an uncanny ability to zero in on the essentials. Most of his photos had a signature starkness to them; all superfluity was cut away. He made the world a simpler, less cluttered place.

They weren't all like that, though. As she spent more time with them, she realized that the sharpness, the singular focus, was a later development. His earlier ones had been busier, more personal.

"Messier," he told her succinctly when she commented on it.

Chloe wasn't sure she agreed, but who could argue with his success? There was no missing a Gibson Walker photo now. They were elementally simple. They focused your eye, told you what to look at, what to think about it when you did.

It was a little like going to a museum and studying the pieces in each exhibit.

Chloe could say that with certainty because when she wasn't looking at Gibson's work, she had spent time at the Museum of Modern Art. She knew there were plenty of wonderful museums in the city, but she began with that one because it seemed the furthest from what she was likely to find in Collierville.

When she got home from work Friday night, though, she sat down on the stoop with the guidebook she'd just bought and began to make plans for the weekend, determined to see as many others as she could.

Rhys appeared, carrying a bag of groceries, and dropped down beside her to offer some suggestions. He even said he would be happy to do some "touristing" with her.

"Really?"

He grinned. "Sure. It will make me appreciate the city if I see it through your eyes. Where do you want to go?"

"How about Ellis Island?"

"Sounds good. Sunday?"

Chloe nodded eagerly. "And on Saturday I'll go to the Metropolitan in the morning and the Frick in the afternoon."

"You'd better take it bit by bit," Rhys advised. "It is possible to overdo."

In the end Chloe decided he was right. So she did her laundry on Saturday morning. And while she sat in the Laundromat waiting for it to finish, she flipped through magazines looking for Gibson's work. It was amazing how much there was—and how easy it was to recognize now that she knew what to look for.

She went to the Metropolitan in the afternoon and discovered that Rhys was right. There was such a thing as visual overload. Eventually she decided she would do better limiting herself to the Egyptians, Greeks and Romans. After all, one of the joys of living in the city was being able to come back whenever she wanted. She didn't have to do the whole museum in a day.

Feeling suitably cultured, she walked back across the park and stopped for dinner in a little Thai place a few blocks from the apartment. Gibson had mentioned how much he liked Thai food the other day. Chloe had never tried it. In Collierville ethnic restaurants weren't thick on the ground.

After her meal, she wished they were. Now Chloe knew she liked Thai food, too.

Would Dave? Maybe she should stop at the bookstore and find a Thai cookbook. Then tonight when she called him, she could tell him about it and say she was going to cook him some.

There was a huge bookstore not far from Lincoln Center. It was in the other direction, but Chloe didn't mind the walk on a warm summer evening. So after she'd eaten, instead of going back to the apartment, she walked down there.

She prowled the cookbook section, found a good half dozen on Thai cooking and finally picked the smallest one with pretty pictures. She wasn't sure she'd convince Dave it was wonderful if she didn't have something to show him.

She was going back down the escalator, book in hand, when a large section of oversize photography books caught her eye.

There were so many, of so many different subjects—people, places, buildings, lifestyles. You named it, and someone had taken pictures of it.

She wondered if Gibson had published any books.

Curious, she began to look. There were even more books on high profile models and the glitzy life than there were on Thai cooking. Chloe was amazed. She worked her way down the aisle, scanning the glossy oversized volumes for Gib's name. Walker, of course, would get him shelved at the bottom.

She got down on her knees and bent her head to look, crawling forward, finding at last a book with the name Walker on the spine. She reached for it.

Someone stepped on her other hand. "Oh, sorry!"

Chloe jerked her hand back, fumbled with the book, clutched it against her, and looked up to see Gibson staring down, astonished, into her face.

"Chloe?" He shoved the book he'd been looking at back onto the shelf, then reached down a hand and hauled her unceremoniously to her feet. "What the hell are you doing down there?"

"Um. Looking at…books. I was wondering if you'd ever published any. So I thought I'd check." She held it up to show him what she'd found, assuming he'd be pleased because she could see now that it was, indeed, a photo study by Gibson Walker.

He didn't look pleased. In fact he was scowling as he looked at the book she held in her hand.

"What the hell are you doing with that?"

"I told you. I've been studying your work. Trying to learn."

"Not from that," he said gruffly. He tried to take it from her, but she didn't let go.

She looked at it now more closely, and her eyes widened when she saw the subject matter. "Catherine Neale? Wow. You did a whole book on her?"

Catherine Neale was one of the most glamorous actresses in Hollywood. But, Chloe remembered now, before she'd moved to the screen, she'd been a model.

"You knew Catherine Neale?"

"Thought I did," Gib muttered. "A long time ago. I'm surprised there's any of the damn things left." He dropped his grip on the book, letting her have it at last. In fact he turned away, as if he didn't care to look at it.

Chloe was torn between looking at it right then and trying to continue talking to Gibson. "Is it the only book you've done?"

"Yeah." Then he glanced over the shelves of books and said derisively, "Not the only one about her, though." He jerked his head toward several more that Chloe could see had Catherine Neale's name on the spine.

One of them, she noted, was the book he'd been looking at. Checking out the competition, was he?

She didn't ask that. Instead she simply said, "She's very photogenic."

"And she knew it." Then he turned back and took the other book out of her hand. "What have you got here?"

She flushed a little, remembering that she'd eaten Thai food because he'd recommended it. But he wouldn't know that, she reminded herself.

"I just had the most wonderful meal..." She told him about it, then said, "I got the book so I could try it at home. For Dave."

Gib's jaw hardened. "Right," he said. "Dave. And you can try it out on the hunky fireman before you go home, can't you?" There was a hard edge to his tone that made Chloe blink.

"What?" She looked at him, confused.

"Nothing." He thrust the book back at her and glanced at his watch. "I've got to go. Got a date."

"Same girl?" Chloe asked, before she could remind herself that it was none of her business.

"What?" He looked almost startled. Then he shook his head. "Oh, no. Never the same girl." A sardonic smile flickered across his face. "Have fun with your cookbook." He turned to leave, then glanced back at Chloe. "Put that back on the shelf," he advised. "It isn't worth your time."

This time when he turned away, he didn't look back. But

Chloe stood watching him until he had gone down the escalator and disappeared from sight. When he had she looked down at the Catherine Neale book again.

Maybe it was old. Maybe it wasn't work he was even very proud of anymore. But she was curious.

What had he meant when he'd said, *Thought I did*?

She took the book and found a fat, overstuffed armchair. There she sat down, tucked her knees under her and began to turn the pages.

She wasn't sure what she expected to find. But whatever it had been, it was far less than what she got.

She got Catherine Neale at her most basic, because this was, after all, a Gibson Walker book.

But she got something more—something personal. In virtually all of the ads and photos she'd studied, Gibson had been ruthless in his focus.

There was nothing ruthless in his portrayal of Catherine Neale. He gave the reader Catherine in her fullness. The pictures were messy and cluttered compared to his later work. But there was a warmth, a personal touch, that he'd carefully excised later on.

The portraits of Catherine showed her as young, fresh, vibrant. She played with the camera as if it were a kitten, teasing it. Clothed in funky artsy outfits, camping it up, she mugged outrageously in some shots; in another she stood silhouetted in an apartment window, looking out at the city, at the stars, at the moon. And there was such longing in her face, such desperation. What had she been thinking? On the next page Chloe learned the answer because Gib had caught her looking just the same way when she stared at a theater marquee.

"Her name in lights," Chloe murmured. That was what she'd longed for.

There were several other shots of Catherine nude—clothed only in shadows or draped in the mussed sheets of an unmade bed. And there her expressions changed. In some she seemed distant, remote, almost, though the camera sought a connection. And in others, she was teasing again, promising...suggesting.

In all of them Chloe could see that she was not yet Catherine Neale, the actress, or Catherine Neale, the movie star. But Gib had found her potential in the way she interacted with the environment and with the camera he held.

Chloe thought he must have shot most of the photos when both he and Catherine Neale were getting started on the careers that would make them each famous.

And in the photos it was possible to see the incipient talent of each.

Catherine exuded star appeal when she was doing nothing more than eating an apple or relaxing in a bubble-filled bathtub. The way she looked at the camera brought to Chloe's mind Eve the temptress.

Had she tempted Gib?

He was certainly impervious to the women who modeled for him now. While he was easy and charming and teasing with them, he never let himself get drawn in. He caught their potential—just as he'd caught Catherine Neale's. But he was never seduced by it.

It was amazing, she thought, how he could do that—how he could remain so detached personally, and yet through his camera could connect with the essence of the person he was taking photos of.

She marveled at it. She wished she could do as well. Her photos of Sister Carmela, catching the abbess at both contemplation and alive with laughter at a funny story, were close. But they weren't anywhere near as good as Gibson's.

"That's why he's the great New York photographer," she told herself, "and you're not."

But she could learn from him. She was learning from him—every day. And now from his book, too.

She closed it now and sat thinking about what it would

be like to do a book like this in-depth study of Catherine Neale that Gibson had done.

He had certainly had access to the details of Catherine Neale's life. She must have trusted him a great deal to give him that much freedom.

Chloe tried to imagine herself doing what Gibson had done—stepping in and chronicling a person's moods, hopes, fears, desires. What would it be like, for example, to know Gibson that well?

She tried to imagine taking photos of him. Of course there would be photos in the studio. After the time she'd spent working with him there, she had a few favorites—poses that seemed to her to capture the essential working Gibson Walker.

She would shoot him behind the camera, moving as he always did. She'd always stood in one place when she was taking her photos. Gibson, she'd learned, was rarely still. He prowled, looking for angles, looking for insights.

Chloe, photographing him, would do the same.

She would shoot him studying the contact sheets, too, catching the almost perennial scowl on his face—and then, she was determined, she would capture that grin of elation that sometimes broke out when he found an image that particularly pleased him.

She would shoot him bossing Misty around, raking his fingers through his hair, scratching the back of his head when he was perplexed about something. She would shoot him looking straight at her, challenging her.

And then, she knew, she would shoot him striding away from her as he had tonight.

And she would follow him—would see him in other settings.

What was Gibson like when he wasn't in his studio? He'd taken her to Mariah's, but she'd never seen where he liked to go. She'd never seen his apartment. What was it like? Was it lavish or spartan? Large or small? What clothes were

in his closet besides the jeans and casual shirts he wore to
work every day? Did he wear boxers? Or briefs?

What did he look like nude?

Nude?

Her eyes jerked open. She glanced at her watch.

Omigod! It was almost ten and she'd forgotten to call
Dave!

Gib thought they'd burned all those old books.

To discover Chloe scrabbling around on the floor with
one in her hand didn't thrill him at all. To have her avidly
curious about it and determined, he was sure, to sit down
and pore over the damn thing was worse.

Worst of all was going back the next day to buy it and
throw it away—to discover it wasn't there.

She hadn't bought it herself, had she?

No, of course not. She didn't have money to throw away
on ridiculous stuff like that. There were only a few die-hard
Catherine Neale fans who would be so devoted or so perverse. Chloe couldn't be counted among them, he was sure.

But she did want to know how to take good pictures.

Every day she did what he told her in the studio. But at
the same time, he knew she was watching what he did as
well.

"It's what I'm here for," she said simply when he re-
marked on it. "I'm here to help, of course. But I'm also
here to learn."

He was fairly sure that, to Chloe, learning probably meant
buying that stupid book. Oh, hell.

But when Monday morning rolled around, she didn't
mention it.

He looked at her warily when she first came in, expecting
that at any moment she would begin to ask about some of
the photos, about Catherine, about how he'd managed to get
so close to such a big star. But she just sat down behind
Edith's desk and started working.

Good, Gib thought. He didn't need her pestering him all morning. She'd ask questions about the book. Or she'd prattle on about whatever museum she went to see. Or she'd talk about dear long-suffering Dave.

He didn't need that.

He was glad she was in the other room.

Before an hour had passed he wanted her back. Misty dropped things. She forgot things. She dithered.

Gib told her to go out and answer the phones and send in Chloe, who knew what she was doing. Misty looked at him as if he'd kicked her. He thought she was lucky he hadn't.

Moments later Chloe came in, shaking her head disapprovingly. "You hurt Misty's feelings."

Gib snorted. He said something short and pithy that turned the tips of Chloe's ears red.

"Your sister should have washed your mouth out more often," she muttered, picking up the reflector that Misty had dropped and checking it for damage.

Gib grinned. "She wouldn't have dared."

"I would have," Chloe said tartly. Her eyes flashed blue fire at him.

Gib laughed, suddenly exhilarated. "I'd like to see you try."

The air fairly crackled with the tension arcing between them. They stood there, eyes locked, breathing hard. Then Chloe's breasts rose. Gib inhaled sharply.

"Are you ready yet?" the model whined.

Gib jerked his gaze away. He snatched up his camera.

"Yeah," he said shortly. "We're ready. Come on, Chloe. Don't just stand there. Get those reflectors set. Hurry up!"

He spared her a quick glance. She blinked, as if she was just coming out of a momentary shock. Then she gave herself a little shake and turned quickly back to work.

They barely said a word to each other for the rest of the afternoon.

* * *

She should never have thought of him naked!

Ever since she had barely been able to talk to him! She could barely look at him—not when he was looking at her, anyway!

And yesterday she'd as good as threatened to wash his mouth out with soap! *She* was the one who needed her mouth washed out—or her imagination!

What was wrong with her?

It was Dave. She was missing Dave. That was the problem.

She was used to having a man to relate to. And since she didn't have Dave here, she naturally, instinctively related to whatever man was around.

It just happened to be Gibson.

Now that she knew, Chloe was determined to take pains to be distant. Remote. Unaware.

Yeah, sure. She shook her head disgustedly, slumped at the desk and buried her face in her hands. To be unaware of Gibson Walker she would have to be dead!

Well, okay. Not unaware, then. But she would be awake and wary.

And engaged.

"Got to keep remembering Dave." She sat up straight and stared at the ring on her finger. The small diamond winked reassuringly at her. "Dave," she murmured. "Dave."

It was good that she was doing Edith's job now. It kept her out of Gib's way—except on days like yesterday when Misty drove him to distraction and he called her in to help him.

Fortunately that wouldn't happen today. Today Gib and Misty were shooting on location in Central Park. They had left at eight. They would be gone all day.

Chloe could breathe easily. Do the filing. Post the bills. Confirm tomorrow's models. Talk to reps who called.

Schedule coming shoots. Deal with whatever came through when the phone rang—as it did now.

"Get the hell up here!" Gib's voice rasped in her ear.

"What?"

"Take a cab to 72nd. Now. I need you."

"I don't—" Chloe began desperately.

"Don't babble. Just do it. I fired Misty. You're my new girl!"

CHAPTER FOUR

WITHOUT Misty to defuse the tension, without Edith to run interference, there were just the two of them working together every day. Being "wary, though aware" simply didn't cut it.

Chloe had to remind herself continually about what really mattered. She had to *talk* about what really mattered.

Dave.

So she did.

All that afternoon while she worked alongside Gibson in Central Park, she talked about how Dave would be just amazed that there, in the center of Manhattan, a person could almost get lost in the woods. The following day she talked about how he would have enjoyed the film she went to see last night.

"Dave and I don't get a chance to see many foreign films," she said. "They don't often play in Collierville."

Gib didn't reply. He just looked at her and rolled his eyes.

"Well, of course, you know that," Chloe went on, aware that she was babbling, but needing to. "But Dave and I like them. Dave especially likes the ones in French. He took French in college. He wanted to go to France during his junior year, but he didn't have the chance. His dad needed help on the farm, so Dave came home instead."

The next day she talked about how good Dave was with his three nephews. It was easy to bring it up because they were shooting an ad with children that day. Girls, of course. Sometimes Chloe wondered if Gib ever shot the male of the species.

But it didn't matter as long as she could think of a way to drag Dave's name into the conversation.

It was helping her, she thought. She wasn't nearly as aware of Gib as she had been after last weekend's encounter in the bookstore. She never thought about photographing him naked anymore.

Well, not often.

Trying *not* to think about it was self-defeating, after all. Like trying *not* to think about blue hyenas. Suddenly they were in every nook and cranny of your mind. Chloe did not want a naked Gibson Walker in every nook and cranny of her mind!

She called Dave every night. She spent most of Thursday evening at South Street Seaport with Rhys. They had made the date during their trip to Ellis Island.

Gib chided her about it when he found out. "Does What's-His-Name approve of you going out with other men?"

"Dave, you mean?" she said, though she knew by now he was doing it to annoy. "Of course."

She couldn't have said why, but her "dates" with Rhys seemed less risky than just thinking about Gibson did.

She didn't pick up the book on Catherine Neale again. She buried it beneath the mattress on the floor of the bedroom the plasterers had finished so she wouldn't have to see it. She didn't want reminders!

Apparently she didn't need them. The next night she found herself dreaming about having a camera and taking pictures of Gibson... No!

She was *not* dreaming about taking pictures of Gibson naked. It was just the...the power of suggestion. So what if it had been her own suggestion?

They were spending too many days together at work—and too many nights together in her mind.

She counted the hours until the weekend.

She needed two whole days in which she would not see Gibson Walker at all.

* * *

He never should have fired Misty.

He should have put up with her bumbling, her fumbling, her spacy dazed expression, her perennial nonsequiturs, her inability to load film. He even should have ignored her having dropped that lens, then picked it up and ground the dirt into it as she "cleaned it off" with her shirt tail.

If he had, he might have had to buy a new lens, but at least he would have had some sanity left by Friday.

But he hadn't. He'd fired Misty and spent the whole week with Chloe—for his sins.

He got to watch her wiggle and jiggle and bounce. He got to feel the brush of those golden curls whenever she slipped past him in the studio. He got to smell the soft flower fragrance of her perfume—of *her*—because she told him when he asked what the hell that smell was that she didn't *wear* perfume. He got to hear hour upon hour of her breathless enthusiasms and eager, endless questions.

Mostly he got hard.

It wasn't a state conducive to good photography. At least not when he was expected to photograph someone else! Lots of someone elses. All week long.

All week long, all he seemed to be aware of was Chloe.

Chloe, for her part, talked only of Dave.

Dave. Dave. Dave.

If she'd babbled on about dear Dave last week, it was nothing compared to this.

Finally, Friday, Gib had had enough.

"Taking up transcendental meditation, are you?" he snapped, scowling at her from behind his camera.

"What?"

"That mantra you're saying over and over. Dave, Dave, Dave."

Chloe's face flushed. "I don't mean to bore you."

"Well, you are. So just shut up about him! I don't want to hear another word. If you're going to prattle on senselessly, I can damned well finish up on my own." He pointed toward the door. "Go out and do Edith's work and leave me alone!"

"That's what I was supposed to be doing all week," Chloe reminded him, blinking rapidly. Her voice seemed steady enough, but her lower lip jutted out and there was hurt in her big blue-violet eyes.

Hell. She wasn't going to cry, was she?

Then Gibson's jaw hardened. So what if she did?

If her feelings were hurt that easily, she just needed to toughen up a bit. She was the one who had wanted to be his assistant. He hadn't asked for her! Resolutely he turned his back on her and went to work.

Only when the last model had left did he consider the possibility of apologizing for his earlier gruffness. It was Friday evening, after all; tempers were bound to be a bit short, he'd tell her. Then he'd buy her dinner and—

Chloe was on the phone.

With a man.

He knew it was a man by the way she was dimpling. She had this way of turning her head, kind of cocking it to the side as she talked—and smiled—and *giggled*!

Damned if she wasn't flirting right there on the office phone!

"I don't pay you to chat with your boyfriend on my time," Gib said sharply, all thought of apologizing gone.

"It's not—"

He cut her off. "I've got work to do in the darkroom. I'll be finishing late. Take off when you're through out here. In the meantime, tell *Dave* to let you get your work done!"

"I wasn't—"

"And leave me alone. I don't want to be disturbed!"

He locked himself in the darkroom and set to work. Time passed. Minutes turned into hours. Once he'd got his focus, he never noticed. The darkroom had always been one of his favorite places. For the ads he did, most of his work was in color. That film he had to send out. But these last rolls had been in black and white and, as such, he got to play with the negatives himself.

He loved that. There was as much creativity possible there as there was behind the camera. It was totally absorbing, totally relaxing.

Especially since he got to focus on some very beautiful women and put one very annoying one right out of his mind.

It was nearly nine when he finally finished. He raked his fingers through his hair and flexed his stiff shoulders. It felt good. *He* felt good. Settled. Well, perhaps not precisely settled, but at least less restless than he had been in weeks— or a couple of weeks, anyway.

He shrugged his shoulders again to get the kinks out, then pushed open the door between the studio and the reception area.

"What the hell are you still doing here?"

Chloe was sitting in the same chair he'd left her in hours ago, clicking away on the computer.

At his sharp words, she looked up and blinked owlishly. "You said to finish. There was a lot to do. I had a lot of Edith's work to do. I was too busy after you fired Misty and—"

So much for settled. He could feel the knot between his shoulders tighten. "You could have finished a long time ago," he accused her, "if you hadn't spent the whole afternoon talking to What's-His-Name!"

"Dave."

"I *know* his name!"

She pressed her lips together. "Well, it wasn't Dave."

"What do you mean it wasn't Dave? Who the hell else do you simper to?"

"I wasn't simpering! I was talking to Rhys. We're having dinner tomorrow. We're cooking Thai."

Gib scowled. He should have found out more about this Rhys character before he let her move into Mariah's. What if the guy was an axe murderer or—worse—some hot-blooded, womanizing Casanova? The sort who got his kicks out of seducing innocents?

He stalked across the room to scowl down at her. "What do you know about him?"

"He's a fireman, like Mariah said. But—" Chloe brightened "—not just a down-the-street-ride-on-a-big-red-truck fireman. He's a specialist. He goes all over the world. He deals with those big out of control blazes like they have when oil wells explode or when earthquakes destroy cities. He just came back from South America..."

She went on, telling Gib all about Rhys Whoever's latest firefighting escapades.

Finally he broke in. "Mariah give you his biography, did she?"

"Mariah? No. I asked him."

"You asked him? When?"

"When we were at Ellis Island. We went there last Sunday."

Gib's frown deepened.

"And then last night when we were doing laundry," Chloe went on.

Ellis Island? That was bad enough. But laundry? *"You were doing laundry with him?"*

Okay, so he was barking at her. She deserved it. What business did she have doing laundry with a perfect stranger? What did she know about the jerk?

"I ran into him as I was going out to the Laundromat, and he said it was crazy to go all the way over there when I could use his washing machine."

Gib groaned.

"What's wrong?"

"He didn't just say, 'Come down and see my etchings, my succulent little lamb?' He couldn't help it if sarcasm dripped from his words.

But Chloe just laughed at him! "He's not going to do something like that. He knows I'm engaged."

As if it were that simple.

Gib shook his head despairingly. "And he's going to remember that?"

"Of course," Chloe said blithely. "And I'm cooking dinner for him on Saturday in exchange."

Just how big an innocent was she? Gib wondered.

Of course it wasn't really any of his business, he reminded himself. And there was no reason at all to get involved. It wasn't his problem if something happened to Chloe Madsen on her foray into the big city.

But Gina had sent her to New York.

His sister would feel responsible if something happened to her, if some hunky fireman took advantage of her.

For his sister's sake, Gib thought maybe he'd do some checking. "What did you say his last name was?"

"I didn't."

He arched a brow, as if to say, *But you will.* He stared at her, giving her his best steely-eyed look.

She stared back. Finally she muttered, "It's Wolfe. Rhys Wolfe."

Wolf.

Gib sighed. It figured.

Chloe had planned a leisurely day on Saturday. She was going to the Empire State Building in the morning. In the afternoon she intended to take a walking tour of Greenwich Village. She had promised Rhys she would be at his place by five to start dinner.

She washed her breakfast dishes and then began to put on her sandals, almost ready to leave when the phone rang.

"I'm putting together a portfolio for a potential client," a gruff male voice said without preamble when Chloe answered.

"What?"

"You heard me. Meet me at the studio in an hour."

There was nothing else—only a click, followed by dead

air—in which Chloe could still hear the reverberations of a voice she recognized all too well.

She stood staring at the receiver in her hand. Then she banged it down.

"Meet me at the studio at noon," she muttered.

Not "please." Not "will you?" Not "I know it's Saturday, but I could use a bit of help." No. Just "Meet me at the studio."

"I shouldn't do it," she mumbled to herself. "I should just ignore it, pretend he got the wrong number."

But she wouldn't, of course.

It was her job to go, to be there, to help. She was Ms. Dependable. Ms. Reliable.

And she really did want to learn. If she spent the day working with Gibson she would learn more than she would on a tour of Greenwich Village. She knew that.

That wasn't the reason she was reluctant to do it.

The reason was Gibson Walker.

The phone call had come last night, out of the blue, surprising Gibson when he'd answered.

"Palinkov here," the lightly accented Russian voice had said. "Dmitri Palinkov. You know?"

Oh, yes, Gibson knew. The whole fashion and advertising world knew about the world's latest designer-sensation. His bold colors and striking lines had caught the eye of everyone in Paris and Milan last year. This year he was doing a collection in New York as well.

"I am looking for a photographer," Palinkov said. "With vision."

Gib's fingers tightened on the receiver. "Vision?"

"Mm. I speak to Marie," Palinkov said. "Kemmerer. You know?"

Yes, Gibson knew Marie, too. Marie Kemmerer was Gibson's agent—one of the best in the business. She wasn't

just a good agent, she was also a woman with "influence."
Marie knew everyone. Marie made "connections."

"Marie, she mention you. I would like to see your best
work. What *you* consider your best work, I mean. It is a
matter of vision, you see. You have a vision. I have a vision.
I look for a photographer for my collection whose vision
can interpret best my own. Marie show me some of your
work. I think...maybe..." he paused "...you are that man.
There are one or two others, I admit," he added quickly.
"I do not know yet. But I want to see the way you think,
what you...how do you say?...value. Then I will know.
Thirty photos, maybe. More or less. You will put something
together for me, yes?"

Yes.

So that was what Gibson was doing in the studio—going
through his work, appraising and assessing, trying to put
together an honest portfolio that would best represent him—
and his view of the world.

To get the biggest, best assignment of his career.

And he just thought Chloe should be part of that process.

She had impressed him. On a purely professional level,
of course. She asked good questions. She had good instincts—*photographic* instincts. Her ability to anticipate his
needs bordered on the amazing, and sometimes she seemed
to know where he wanted things before he even spoke. She
understood a little of his vision. He knew she'd been studying his work. It would be good to have her there.

And if she was a little late cooking dinner with Rhys the
Wolf, well, that wasn't all bad, either.

So he called her. Then had immediate second thoughts.
Then shrugged them off.

They all came flooding back when a very primal sexual
awareness crackled between them the minute she walked in
the door and glared at him.

"What?" Gib demanded, offended and defensive at the

same time. "You're mad because I made you come in to work today?"

"Of course not. I just—you could have asked."

He grunted. He could have. He rarely did. Besides, if he had, she might have said no. Since he hadn't she was here.

"Did I interrupt something?" he challenged. "An afternoon tryst with the wolfman?"

Her eyes widened for an instant, then narrowed. "I am cooking Rhys dinner," she said flatly. "That's all. I am engaged. To Dave."

She thumped his name down between them like a gauntlet. Gib could almost hear it hit. They glared at each other for a full minute.

Finally he sucked in a sharp breath and jerked his head toward the back room. "Come on. We've got work to do."

Before she arrived, Gib had dragged folios and boxes of old photos and tear sheets out of the cupboards. Now he spread them on the table. As he did, he told her about Palinkov's phone call, about his work as a designer, about what he wanted from Gibson.

"I'm supposed to give him an understanding of my vision," he said. "What I see. What I capture. What I do best."

Chloe's curls bobbed. She nodded seriously.

He began pulling out his strongest photos. The ones that had got him acclaim, the ones people stopped and stared at. The ones that had made his name.

Chloe looked them over, paused over this one, stopped and studied that one. She put some on one pile, some on another.

Gib pulled out more.

"We need stacks for types of feelings," Chloe told him, moving to stand beside him.

He caught a hint of that flower scent again. He stiffened. But he was oddly reluctant to move away.

"Here." Chloe slipped a hand beneath his and took the

photos he was holding. She began sorting them. He
watched. He wasn't looking at the photos. He was breathing
carefully—and looking at Chloe.

Her head was bent as she went through the photos. She
was paying no attention to him at all.

She made several piles, then pulled out a few. "Look at
these," she said.

They weren't as striking as the ones he'd picked. They
didn't shout his vision. They were quieter, subtler. Gentler.

He shook his head. "They don't grab you. Palinkov's
stuff grabs you."

"He wants *your* vision," Chloe argued.

Gib gestured toward the harder edged photos. "They're
my vision."

"But not all of it."

"These—" Gib indicated the ones she'd picked
"—aren't as good as those."

She studied the photos again, then nodded. "You're right.
But," she said, "you do have some like this that are as
good."

"Which? What do you mean?"

"In your Catherine Neale book."

Gib's jaw snapped shut. He shook his head. "No."

"They're softer. Fuller."

"No."

"They're as good as these you picked."

"Damn it, I said, *no!*"

She lifted her gaze and looked at him. He glared at her
for a long moment, then deliberately turned away.

"Those were very good photos, Gib," she said quietly.
"They show an entirely different side of you. An intimate
side. They're another way you see."

"They were a way I *saw*," he corrected sharply. "Not
anymore."

She cocked her head. "What? Not ever?"

He shook his head. "Never," he said firmly.

But Chloe didn't accept that. "I thought they were good. They showed so much—seemed to understand so much—"

"Damn it, just drop it! Look—" he thrust a pile of more recent ad photos at her "—this is the stuff Palinkov will want to see. These are the fashion photos. This is The Look. Study it. Pick some. Then we'll compare."

Dutifully Chloe took them from him. She carried them over to the desk on the far side of the studio. "I'll just sort through them here," she said, keeping her back to him.

"Do that," Gib muttered.

It was better that way. Better they didn't try to work together. Obviously she wasn't as perceptive as he thought. She couldn't see how much he'd improved since the Catherine Neale book. He poked through the stack of photos he had, laying them, as she'd suggested, in piles. Then he took each pile in turn and set two photos against each other, choosing the better. He worked in silence.

So did she.

They worked all afternoon. Picking, sorting, deliberating. At one point Gib came across the ones he'd taken the day Chloe had arrived. He hadn't looked at them since that day.

Had been sorely tempted. Hadn't done it.

But now, hell, it was in the line of work, wasn't it? He stood with his hands braced, palms flat on the table, as he stared down at them.

They were…different.

She was different.

All the other girls looked smooth, practiced, flawless, untouchable.

Chloe looked…lovely.

She looked alive. Gib could almost see her bouncing. He swallowed. His body tightened. He dropped his head and took a long, careful breath.

"Oh, no!" said a voice right behind him. "You're *not* putting in one of those!"

He turned, grinning, to see a hectic flood of color in Chloe's face. She was glaring at him.

"Put those away! Or better, throw them out!" She tried to reach around him to get at them. He stepped in front of them to block her access.

She moved. So did he, staying between her and the photos, still grinning.

"Gibson! Give them—"

He shook his head. "No."

She feinted one way, then tried to slip a hand past him on the other side. He lurched one way, then back, then caught her hand.

Their bodies bumped and Chloe's breasts came up against the wall of Gib's chest.

Time stopped.

Everything stopped—except the thunder of their hearts. And the desperate blinking of Chloe's eyes as she stared helplessly up into his. Her bottom lip trembled, and Gib bent his head to touch it with his own.

But then, before he could, she jerked away, out of his grasp, stumbled backwards and caught herself against the chair. "Don't," she whispered, lashes still fluttering, though the command seemed as much directed at herself as at him, Gib thought.

It didn't matter.

They wouldn't. The moment was past. The insanity had fled.

"I—I've got to go," Chloe mumbled, straightening up away from the chair, brushing obviously shaking hands down the legs of her slacks. She didn't look at him, just backed away. "I...promised Rh-Rhys..."

Gib's teeth came together with a snap. But he didn't reply. Didn't know what he'd say if he opened his mouth. Finally he nodded his head. "Right," he said, his voice a little ragged, but at least hard-edged. "You do that." He made it sound like a dismissal. "Go on. I can finish up."

Jerkily Chloe nodded. She knotted her fingers together, as if she didn't know what to do with her hands. Then she tipped her head toward the desk where she'd been working. "I...put some good ones in a stack over th-there. Ones I think you sh-should use."

"Thanks."

She started toward the door. Stopped. Looked back over her shoulder at him. "Don't use those photos, Gib. Please."

The ones of her, she meant. She bit her lip and looked at him beseechingly.

"They're good." He couldn't help saying it. Most women he knew would be begging him to put their picture in front of a man the caliber of Dmitri Palinkov.

God knew Catherine had.

But Chloe just shook her head miserably. "Not...for me. Please." Again her lashes fluttered. But there was nothing calculated about it. She wasn't putting on any act. She looked as if she might cry.

Gib didn't deal with crying women. He shrugged irritably. "I won't," he conceded gruffly after a moment.

A smile the like of which he'd never seen lit Chloe's face. "Thank you, Gib." And then she flew across the room and planted a kiss right on his mouth.

They both jumped back as if a thousand volts of electricity had jolted between them.

Chloe clapped her hand to her mouth and whispered a shocked, "I'm sorry!"

Then, leaving Gib staring numbly after her, she fled.

She was an idiot!

A fool!

A first-class imbecile!

How could she have done something so stupid? Why on earth had she kissed Gibson Walker?

She must be nuts!

All the way back to the apartment, Chloe's mind reeled

with the memory of that kiss. It would have had enough reeling to do with the simple buzz that had arced between them when he'd grabbed her as she'd tried to get the photos away from him and their bodies had touched.

The tension between them had been palpable. Sexual. Downright scary. The room had simply seemed to sizzle with it. She'd been right to turn and run.

And a damn fool to come back and kiss him when he'd promised not to use the photographs!

She sank down on the seat in the subway train, pressed her hands over her eyes and simply quaked. Then she took deep cleansing breaths and dragged her palms down her clammy cheeks and stared at her reflection as it bounced off the windows opposite as the train rattled along.

She tried to see something there that would explain the idiocy of her action, some sign in her face that would explain why she had done such a thing. But all she could see was confusion.

And desire.

She pressed her hands over her eyes again.

"Dave," she murmured. "Dave." Again. More desperately. "Dave!"

She forgot to get off at 79th Street. The train reached 86th before she was aware of it. She got off there and walked back, praying for sanity and composure as she did so.

"Thought you'd forgotten," Rhys said cheerfully when she knocked on his door.

"S-sorry I'm late," Chloe babbled as he ushered her in. "I...had to work."

"It's Saturday! What kind of a slave driver is he?"

"He's...not. N-not exactly."

Rhys's brows lifted. Then he shrugged. "Oh, yeah. I forgot. He's the hot-shot photographer of beautiful women, isn't he?'' He shook his head. "Makes them bare their souls as well as their bodies?''

Chloe felt her cheeks go scarlet.

Rhys took one look at her and laughed. "Got you under his spell?''

"He does not!''

But he certainly had done something to her. She was supposed to have come to New York to broaden her horizons, not to kiss Gibson Walker!

Not to lose her mind—and her common sense!

He'd been too long without a woman.

That was all it was. Hormones.

He'd been too absorbed in his work for too damn long. It was clouding his judgement, making him susceptible, subverting his common sense.

He'd get a woman.

It wouldn't be hard to get a woman. They were everywhere—all smiling at him, cooing at him, batting lashes at him. *Wanting him*—and what his photos could do for them.

Yeah? Well, so what?

He didn't care. Let them use him and he'd use them. Tit for tat. You scratch my back and I'll scratch yours. Good business. Common sense.

And it would get his mind off Chloe Madsen.

She was driving him nuts.

What the hell had she kissed him for?

Hadn't she felt the tension in his body when they'd touched? Hadn't she seen the fire in his eyes, the burn across his cheekbones, the tightness in his face?

Didn't she know arousal when she saw it? *Felt* it?

What the hell was the matter with her?

Gib ground his teeth. He knew what was the matter with her. She was missing *Dave*!

If his mind could have spat, it would have spat the name of Chloe's fiancé. Damn the man! He had no sense. Why had he let her come to New York? The woman was lethal! She could drive a saint to sin.

And God knew Gibson was no saint!

He had to get her out of here. Had to get rid of her. Had to get his life back under control.

But until he could do that, he needed a woman.

He stalked into the reception room and began flipping through Edith's phone file. Who could he call? Who wouldn't read into it more than he wanted her to?

Tasha?

No.

Vanessa?

No.

Shellie?

No.

Cards flipped past. Visions of one beautiful woman after another flickered through his mind.

Tina?

No.

Jessica?

No.

Alana.

Alana!

Dark, sultry looks. High cheekbones. Full lips that curled in a sneer more often than a smile. Alana was the antithesis to Chloe. She was svelte. Contained. Starkly beautiful. And absolutely determined that no man was going to be more than her plaything.

Perfect.

Gibson picked up the phone.

CHAPTER FIVE

CHLOE had a nice dinner with Rhys Wolfe.

He was fun, witty and charming—and no threat at all to her engagement to Dave.

Not that he didn't like women; clearly he did. But he didn't like attachments any more than Gibson apparently did. He made that very clear, too, when they cleaned up after dinner.

Chloe said something about how nice it was to find a man who could wash dishes, and then casually asked him why some lucky female hadn't snapped him up.

"Because I'm not for snapping," he told her quite firmly. "I don't do marriage."

There was something so flat and uncompromising about Rhys's words that she knew he wasn't kidding.

She sensed that an invisible shield had dropped, and however curious she was, however much she might have liked to know, she wasn't going to be able to ask him any more than she could ask Gibson. Anyway, neither of them were any of her business.

But wondering about Rhys didn't keep her awake at night.

Gibson did.

Thinking about who he might be dating now irritated her, niggled at her mind, made her toss and turn. Had he ever dated Catherine Neale?

She was willing to bet he had. She tried to remember what she had read about the actress. She was married, Chloe recalled, to a producer. Before that she'd been married to a director. But Gib had known her a long time ago. She'd probably been single then.

It didn't matter, she told herself. Catherine Neale was, as Gib himself said, "a long time ago."

Even if he had once dated her, he'd moved on.

He was clearly eager to be out of the studio early on Monday night. "Got a dinner engagement," he told them. And he almost seemed to be smirking when he said it. He even seemed to swagger a bit.

"Hot date, is it?" Sierra said with a grin.

"Hot date," Gib agreed in a smoky voice, and he shot a sidelong glance toward Chloe, almost as if he wanted to see her reaction.

She didn't react at all. She pretended not to notice. She'd tried all day not to notice Gib!

She didn't want to think about him. Didn't want to remember Saturday. *Refused* to remember what it had been like to kiss his lips!

"Anyone we know?" Sierra asked him as they went down in the elevator.

Gibson's mouth curved into a slow, sexy smile. "Alana."

"Alana?" Sierra's brows shot up as the elevator doors opened. "She'll eat you alive!"

Gib's grin widened. "And I'll enjoy every minute of it."

Then, with a self-satisfied nod, he held the front door so they could precede him out onto the sidewalk, then sketched them a quick salute and strode off briskly, hailing a cab.

Watching him go, Chloe felt oddly hollow. "Who's Alana?"

Sierra pointed at the billboard on the side of the building at the end of the block. It was a thirty-foot-high black-and-white portrait of the slinkiest, sultriest, poutiest, most sensational woman who'd ever hawked an ounce of perfume. "Her."

"Oh," Chloe said. "I see."

"Well, of course," she added just a little feebly. Then

she mustered up a smile from somewhere south of her toe-nails. "How...nice."

Sierra sniffed. "Won't last."

Chloe didn't think so either. After all, he'd once told her, "Never the same one twice."

But Alana lasted.

For more than a day. For more than a week.

Gibson came in every morning, yawning and red-eyed, asked Chloe smugly if she'd had a nice chat with Dave the night before. Then he stretched his arms over his head and mumbled something about being so-o-o tired, and then let drop some comment about his evening with Alana.

She didn't think it was her imagination that was turning the evenings with Alana into "nights."

But she certainly had no intention of asking!

"Yes," she always said as airily as she could, "Dave and I had a lovely chat. Dave..."

But Gib never listened. He always turned away, going deep into whatever shoot he was doing that day, barking orders, moving at top speed, and making Chloe move right along with him.

Twice that week they went to Central Park and shot on location. Three cameras, umpteen fill lights and baffles and reflectors. Not to mention five models with hair more jungly than the flora.

"A challenge," Sierra called it.

Chloe found it a challenge, too. And not just because when they were outside she had to lug heavy power packs with her as well as do all the other to-ing and fro-ing that Gibson required. Mostly because it was a week of swelter-ingly humid days that the city in summer was noted for and Gibson, to cool off, stripped off his shirt while he worked.

He had, Chloe noted, a rather nicely hair-roughened, well-muscled chest.

Not that she cared. Not that she even looked twice!

She wasn't interested in Gibson's chest. Not at all. Not in any man's chest but Dave's.

Dave's.

Dave.

She shut her eyes and cleared her throat. "When Dave and I—"

"Bring me that lens," Gib barked. "Don't just stand there!"

Chloe glared. At him. At his chest. She didn't just stand there, either. She marched right over and slapped the lens into his hands.

And if she stepped on his toes, well, it wasn't her fault Gibson Walker's feet were as big as his ego.

It had nothing to do with him dating Alana.

It wasn't as if she cared.

She didn't. Not a bit. Gibson was a normal, healthy, hot-blooded male, after all. He *should* date.

She just wished he wouldn't talk about it—about *her*—all the time!

But he did. Every day. All day.

Alana was such a great dancer, he said. Alana was so-o-o-o clever, he said. Alana knew how to make a man happy.

Chloe wanted to clap her hands over her ears so she wouldn't have to listen to the Alana this...Alana that... nonsense coming out of Gib's mouth.

Frankly, Chloe thought, Gibson must have *Alana* tattooed on his brain.

She was certainly tattooed all over every other surface in New York!

Everywhere she turned, it seemed, Alana—didn't the woman have a last name, for crying out loud?—was pouting in her face.

On billboards, in magazines, in subway trains. Everywhere Chloe looked, two-dimensional Alanas thrust their sexy lower lip at her.

Then suddenly, one afternoon, the three-dimensional one walked into the office.

"What's *she* doing here?" Chloe said before she could swallow the words.

"She's come to do a shoot," Sierra said. "You booked her two weeks ago."

"Oh." Chloe felt a little red-faced. "That's all right, then," she mumbled to herself. When she'd booked Alana, she hadn't a clue who she was. Things had changed. A lot.

Alana was devastatingly beautiful in her photos, despite the petulant pout. In person she was even more beautiful. For one thing, she wasn't pouting.

In fact she was laughing when she came into the reception area with two other models. The others waggled their fingers at Gib, who was on the telephone, but who nodded at them in acknowledgment. Alana apparently wanted more than an acknowledgment. She went right up and hugged him, then kissed him on the mouth.

Chloe's jaw dropped. She'd seen several hundred air kisses since she'd arrived in New York. In fact that was the only kind of kissing she'd seen, which was what, in retrospect, made her own kiss even more mortifying.

She hadn't realized that "real" kisses just weren't done in New York.

Yeah, well, tell Alana that, Chloe thought.

Then she stared, stupefied, as Gibson kissed Alana right back. Chloe's teeth came together with a snap. How professional was that! She glared her indignation at Gib.

He noticed and gave her a self-satisfied smile. Then, as if he intended to rub it in, he kissed Alana lightly once more. "Hey, sweetheart. How's my girl?"

"Glad to see you," Alana purred. "But running a little late. I've got to meet Walter for drinks in an hour."

Chloe waited for Gib to tell Alana that Walter, whoever he was, would just have to wait. He didn't rush things for anyone. She'd heard him say that often enough since she'd arrived.

But he only nodded and said, "Let's get this show on the road. Chloe," he barked at her. "Snap to."

Chloe's jaw dropped. *"Me?"* As if she were the one holding things up! As if she hadn't been working her tail off all day!

She made the sound of a strangled scream somewhere deep in her throat, then gave him her best obsequious smile. "Yes, boss. Sure, boss. Three bags full, boss."

"What?" Gib frowned.

But Chloe spun on her heel and strode into the studio where she set to work getting the cameras ready.

When Gib sauntered in with his arm around Alana, Chloe glared. Had they been welded at the hip? First it was kisses, now their bodies were crushed together.

Not that she cared, of course. It was just so... so...immature.

How would it look if she threw her arms around Dave and kissed him right in the middle of the office of the *Collierville Gazette*?

Well, she just wouldn't think about it. What Gibson did wasn't important to her except insofar as it had to do with photography. Still, it rankled to watch him fawn all over Alana.

"It doesn't mean anything," Sierra said.

Chloe shrugged. "It doesn't matter to me."

But when Gibson closed the studio early saying he had "another engagement" which was obviously tagging along after Alana to have drinks with Walter, Chloe was annoyed.

Gibson shrugged off her obvious irritation. "More time for you to sightsee," he told her blithely. "Or—" he smiled "—call Dave."

Chloe managed her brightest smile. "What a good idea. I'll just go home and do that."

Dave wasn't there. She'd forgotten the time difference

again. He would be out in the fields still, making hay while the sun shone—literally. And then he'd have to do the milking.

"Fine," Chloe muttered. She'd call Dave later. But she had to do something now! Mariah's apartment was far too small to contain her sudden restlessness. She went back outside to wander around the neighborhood.

Rhys's apartment door opened as she passed. "Hey, what's up?"

"Not much. Just got off work a little early today and thought I'd go wander around."

"Want some company?"

"Sure," she said. "Why not?"

It was perverse that Rhys didn't strike near the sparks off her that Gibson did. Rhys was mellow, pleasant, easy company. She laughed with him, joked with him, thoroughly enjoyed her evening—including a delightful dinner—with him.

Rhys was as restful and relaxing as Gibson was not.

It was a pity, she thought as they walked back to the brownstone later that evening, that he was a smoke jumper—or whatever you called those men who risked their lives jumping into fires to quell them from the inside out. There was no way she was going to get mixed up with a man who did something like that.

It was bad enough with a photographer whom other women salivated over on a daily basis—and who salivated over them.

Suddenly, right there in the middle of Amsterdam Avenue, Chloe stopped.

"What's wrong?" Rhys demanded. "What's the matter?"

She shook her head almost frantically. "N-nothing. Nothing at all." She wetted her lips and smiled, then sucked in a deep breath that wasn't nearly as restorative as she'd hoped. "I just…had a thought."

A terrible thought.

A thought about Gib. She had spent the last block comparing Rhys with Gibson Walker.

She hadn't thought about Dave at all.

Gibson whistled all morning.

When he didn't whistle, he hummed. When he wasn't humming *or* whistling, he seemed to burst into little snatches of song.

Chloe wanted to strangle him. Why didn't he just concentrate on work?

Why did he have to act so blinking happy all the time?

Well, she suspected she knew why. Alana. But damned if she was going to ask!

It didn't matter. Once he stopped humming, whistling and singing, he told her anyway. "Now there's some place you ought to go," he told her. "Ricardo's. Great food. Wonderful atmosphere. Very Italian. Very folksy. Very.. intimate." His voice dropped, caressing that last word.

"I don't think I would find it very intimate," Chloe replied sharply, rooting around in a drawer for a pair of scissors, "unless Dave was here to go with me."

Gibson's jaw hardened slightly. But then he took a breath and went right on. "They have this wonderful little loft with these very private booths. Very private..."

Chloe could just imagine. She slammed the drawer shut.

Sierra, who was fixing the hair of the teenage girls Gibson was shooting that morning for an adolescent skin cream ad, looked up, then rolled her eyes at Gib's deliberately "hungry-male-on-the-prowl" expression, and grinned at Chloe.

Chloe managed a grin in return. It wasn't as easy as she wished.

"Well, I just thought you might want to check it out sometime," Gib went on casually, "in case lover boy ever does make it to the big city."

"I'll consider it," Chloe said tightly.

"But I suppose you'd be better off sticking to museums and Broadway plays on your own." He cocked his head. "Doing a lot of museums and plays, are you?"

Was he baiting her?

And if so, why?

A quick glance at Sierra proved her to be equally intrigued. Having Sierra as a witness, not to mention a pair of agog teenage girls, made Chloe just a little more reckless than she might have been otherwise. Especially now that she could see a glint in his eye.

She lifted her chin and, just as her father always claimed she did, she led with it. "You might be right," she said. "Rhys might like it. I suppose Rhys and I could go."

"Rhys!" The glint in Gib's eyes turned into a glare. "What the hell would you go there with Wolfe for?"

"Why not?" Chloe gave an offhand shrug. "Rhys is always up for new things." She twisted the last words, dangling them, aware, even as she did so, of how they would be interpreted.

Gib looked disgusted. "Poor Dave," he said. "What a chump."

Chloe's brows drew down. "What do you mean, 'poor Dave?' What do you mean, 'What a chump?'"

"Well, he is, isn't he? Staying at home tending his fields while his property's off being poached?"

Chloe stared at him, her mouth opening and closing like a fish's. Sierra and the girls seemed pretty astonished, too. They were looking from Gibson to her and back, as if they were watching a tennis match.

Chloe sputtered. "Property? You think Dave's a chump? You think I'm 'property to be poached?'" Her voice rose unsteadily.

A sardonic smile touched Gibson's mouth. "Well, he can't be too bright, can he? Or he'd never have let you just take off like this," he drawled.

"I didn't 'take off.' I took a job. And I told you before Dave trusts me!"

Gib sneered. "The more fool he, obviously."

"A dinner date does not imply falling into bed with the person at the end of the evening!"

Gib lifted a brow. "No?"

"Don't judge *me* by your own behavior! Just because you seem to consider sex a nightcap after a dinner date doesn't mean that everyone does!"

"Bothers you, does it?" Gib grinned. "Me and Alana in the sack."

Chloe felt as if flames were coming out of her ears. She drew a deep breath and said as sweetly as she could manage, "As much as it bothers you that I had dinner with Rhys."

They glared at each other.

Sierra burst out laughing.

They both whipped around and turned their scowls on her.

"What?" Chloe demanded.

"Something funny?" Gib snarled.

Sierra smothered her laughter, then wiped a hand across her face, leaving it totally inexpressive. "Nothing. Not a thing."

Chloe sniffed. Gib snorted. They went back to work.

Sierra's lips were still twitching as she went back to combing out the model's hair.

He didn't get the Palinkov job.

Gibson couldn't believe it. It was impossible. His vision *was* Palinkov's vision. His women were the bright, bold, striking women that Palinkov designed his clothes for. He was sure of it. They were the women—the photos—he'd chosen.

But Palinkov's words still echoed in his ears, and the receiver still hung from his fingers long after the man himself had hung up.

"I'm sorry," Palinkov had said. "I thought... When Marie showed me...you know, I really thought... But there is something...something missing. A softness, I think you would say."

"Softness?" Gib had repeated, dazed. "What do you mean?"

"It is a part of woman," Palinkov explained. "The caring. The openness. Marie had one or two photos. Early ones, she said. But I did not see it in the photos you sent me."

"I—"

"You are not proud of the soft ones, yes?"

"No. I...don't know. I thought..." But he couldn't think. Didn't want to!

"You are afraid of softness?"

"Of course not."

"I think maybe..." Palinkov's voice trailed off. "You do not know..."

"I know women."

"Yes, yes," Palinkov agreed quickly. "It is yourself, perhaps," he said, "that you do not know."

"What?"

"You are not married?"

"That's right," Gib said through his teeth.

"Ah."

What the hell did that mean? Ah? What was *ah*?

"Marriage teaches a lot."

"You think a photographer has to be married to take good photos?" Gib hoped he didn't sound as incredulous as he felt.

"Not for everything. For this. For my collection."

"Marriage has nothing to do with it. Your colors are bold. Striking. Your designs are simple. Straightforward. What you see is what you get. That's what I do."

"It's what I *did*. A designer does not stay the same. A designer grows. Learns. I learn. I marry. I am more open. My wife, she shows me. Things are not so simple. Life is complex. Full. Some of those photos Marie shows me...I think you see that.'' He sighed. ''But no.''

Gib ground his teeth.

''For my collection, the photographer, he has to know the fullness of being female.''

Why don't you hire a bloody woman, then? Gib almost said the words. Only bare civility kept them in his head.

''Has to appreciate them, trust them, love them. Or one at least,'' Palinkov qualified. ''So I am sorry, Mr. Walker. I regret we will not be working together. But I really think Finn MacCauley and I will—''

''*MacCauley?*''

Palinkov was going to work with Finn MacCauley? Finn MacCauley had beat him out?

Yes, that was what Palinkov had said. Finn MacCauley, Gib's biggest rival, his fiercest competitor, had beat him out!

Now, finally, Gib crashed the phone into the cradle and slammed his palms flat on the desk. ''Damn!'' he said. ''Damn!'' And, ''Damn!'' again.

He said a few other things as well about Palinkov and about Finn, and he finished by throwing himself back onto the sofa and muttering aloud, ''It's all her fault.''

Chloe, he meant.

It was all Chloe Madsen's fault.

If he hadn't been so aware of thinking about her all the time, if he hadn't been so furious that his every waking thought seemed in some way to be connected to Chloe Madsen, he would have chosen different photos.

He might have even put in some of those old ones of Catherine. They had, just as she'd said, captured a different vision. They'd spoken of love and warmth and openness and gentleness.

Just because they meant betrayal to him didn't mean they were bad.

In fact, he realized now, his refusal to include them was less to do with Catherine than to do with Chloe.

She evoked the same response in him. She cracked defenses he'd thought so well built that no one could get in. And now, in his furious effort to shove Chloe out of his mind, he'd shoved out part of his work—and ruined his chance to get Palinkov's job as well.

Damn.

Damn Chloe.

Waving Alana in her face wasn't enough. She was playing havoc with his life—professional as well as personal. He was going to have to send her back to Iowa.

Too bad if her "restlessness" wasn't assuaged yet.

Too bad if she hadn't seen every blinking museum and tried every ethnic restaurant in Manhattan. Too bad if she had to go home and act like someone's fiancée instead of sashaying around Gib's studio with her bouncing curls and her swinging hips and her kissable lips, driving him to distraction.

Too damn bad.

He was going to get rid of her.

He'd promised Gina he wouldn't throw her out. He couldn't just walk in on Monday and fire her, as much as he'd like to.

So he would have to get her to quit. He'd have to scare her into leaving.

How?

By making a play for her himself.

The simplicity of it was breathtaking. And tempting as well.

After all, she was playing with fire anyway, spending all his time with Rhys. If she thought she was so immune, let her come up against a master.

He didn't let himself think about what his sister would say if she got wind of his intentions. So it wasn't proper, appropriate behavior? So it was dirty, underhanded, and maybe, just maybe, even a little cruel?

Too bad.

Gib wasn't a saint. He was a man. A man in desperat[e] need of a little self-preservation.

"Dave trusts you, sweetheart?" he muttered. "Let's se[e] about that."

"Go where?" Chloe blinked at Gib. She'd been trying t[o] stay well away from him all day.

She'd spent almost the entire weekend on the phone wit[h] Dave—chatting about the wedding, making plans, deter[-] minedly *not* letting herself think about anyone else.

She thought she'd done rather well, and she'd come bac[k] to work this morning feeling brisk and businesslike, an[d] certain that she had things well under control.

And now he was asking her to go with him to a party?

"Why?" she asked suspiciously.

He gave her a look of bland innocence. "Why not? I ju[st] thought you'd enjoy it. Get to see a little different wor[ld] than you're used to. Isn't that the point of this whole ex[-] ercise? Seeing how the other half lives so you can go hom[e] and feel satisfied with your choice?"

There was almost, but not quite, an edge to his voice. Sh[e] looked at him closely, trying to tell if he was baiting he[r.] But his expression didn't change. It was still calm and equ[a-] ble, as if he were offering her no more than a sandwich o[n] a plate and not caviar and oysters Rockefeller on Limoge[s.]

"Marie Kemmerer's party?" Sierra's eyes were wide. "[Is] that where he's inviting you?"

Chloe had forgotten the name as soon as he'd said it. B[ut] Gibson nodded.

Sierra looked impressed. "You ought to do that," sh[e] said. "That won't just be a party. It'll be An Event!"

Chloe didn't like the sound of that. "An event?" she sai[d] cautiously. "What kind of event?"

"Marie Kemmerer is his agent. She's famous for her pa[r-] ties," Sierra told her. "She knows everyone. And—" Sier[ra] grinned "—she knows just who to invite to get the best explosions."

"Explosions?" That didn't sound good at all.

Sierra laughed. "Oh, you know. Marie likes things to sizzle. She likes people to buzz. To talk. And she knows how to make it happen. It'll be a blast."

"Have you ever been?"

Sierra shook her head. "I wish."

Chloe looked at Gibson. "Take Sierra."

He didn't so much as glance Sierra's way. "I'm inviting you."

"Why? Can't Alana come?" She didn't know what made her ask that. The minute the words were out of her mouth, she regretted them. She didn't want to sound catty—or jealous. She was *not* jealous!

A grin tipped the corner of his mouth. "No, more's the pity," he drawled. "She's in Texas doing a shoot until a week from Monday."

So he would have taken her if she'd been around. Chloe didn't know why the notion deflated her. It wasn't as if she cared.

"Go," Sierra urged her. "Then you can tell me about it."

"I don't have anything to wear to a party like that."

"You can wear jeans if you want," Gib said. "Marie won't care."

"I can't wear jeans!"

Gib shrugged negligently. "Well, it's not a big deal. You can find something. Sierra could help you."

"Yes," Sierra said eagerly. "Come on, Chloe. It'll be fun."

Fun? That wasn't how Chloe would have described it. She liked New York City, but so far she'd seen it entirely on her own terms. She hadn't been flung into anything social over her head—unless you counted working for Gibson in the first place.

"You can tell Dave," Sierra said. "He'll think it's really neat."

He would very likely think it was silly beyond belief. Dave liked down-home family get-togethers. There was plenty of combustibility right there, he'd have said. He wouldn't go looking for more. But, Chloe realized, she had when she'd decided to come to New York.

She remembered Sister Carmela saying that she had gone out in the world to challenge herself. "It makes me firmer and more determined in my vocation," she'd said, "knowing what I know, seeing what I've seen."

Sister Carmela would go to Marie Kemmerer's.

Chloe sighed. "All right."

It was a kind thing to do, inviting her to go with him to Marie's party.

Friendly. Gentlemanly.

His sister even said so.

"How sweet of you to think of her," Gina enthused on Wednesday evening when she rang him up to see how things were going on.

"They're going fine," he told her, and then he told her what he'd done.

"Wonderful," she said. "How thoughtful of you, Gib."

"That's me," he muttered. "Thoughtful to the end."

"You are, Gib. Truly. You're the dearest man."

He rubbed the back of his neck, feeling uncomfortable, telling himself he had no reason to be. It was a straightforward invitation. No more, no less.

So he wasn't going to feel guilty about it. He wasn't going to feel as if he was throwing her to the wolves. It was what she wanted—an "experience." It would be that, all right. And it would be good for her!

And him.

He reckoned she'd be on the plane to Iowa within days after it.

"Marie is your agent? The one who knows everyone? Well, Chloe will certainly have something to talk about when she gets home, won't she?"

Gib concurred. "Oh, yes."

Not that he figured she would talk about it. She probably wouldn't even want to remember it. Not too closely, anyway. Going to one of Marie Kemmerer's parties was a little bit like flying too close to the sun. A rarified atmosphere if there ever was one.

You had to be damned wary, lest you get burned.

Gib wouldn't let Chloe get badly burned. He just wanted her scorched a bit.

And he was going to enjoy doing a little of the scorching.

CHAPTER SIX

"THIS is a mistake."

It was the hundredth time Chloe had said those words that afternoon, the thousandth—at least—that she'd thought them since Gib had proffered his invitation to accompany him to Marie Kemmerer's party Saturday evening. "I shouldn't go."

"Nonsense," Sierra said just as she had the previous ninety-nine times. "Of course you're going. You're just nervous. But once you get there, you'll have a great time. You'll dazzle them all. Wearing that, how could you not? It's a fantastic dress, if I do say so myself."

It was, Chloe agreed, a fantastic dress.

It was unlike anything she'd ever worn in her entire life. It looked like something right off a Paris runway, she'd said when she'd first seen it.

"It is right off a Paris runway," Sierra had informed her. "Delia wore it there last fall."

It was a designer original. A dress that a model friend of Sierra's had been given by a designer who found slight imperfections in it. "Enjoy," he'd said.

But Delia, six weeks pregnant, had never been able to. She hadn't minded a bit that Chloe would enjoy it instead. "Fine by me," she'd told Sierra. "I'm never going to fit into it again."

Chloe hadn't thought she would either. "I don't have a model's figure," she'd protested when Sierra had brought it by the apartment.

But Sierra had insisted. "Try. I can sew. We'll alter it."

"Delia—"

"Delia won't care. She doesn't even look good in red."

The dress was red. It wasn't just red. It was *red*. There were, granted, a few little tropical flowers scattered here and there—hints of peacock and yellow. But the overwhelming impression was *red*.

"I don't wear red," Chloe had protested even as Sierra had tugged it over her head and pulled it down. It had slid on like the skin of a silken snake, then flared slightly from the hips.

Sierra's eyes had gone saucerlike. "You do now," she'd breathed.

Adamantly Chloe had shaken her head. "I can't! It's obscene! It's shows every curve."

Sierra had nodded cheerfully. "It does that."

"Well, I can't wear it! It's too...too...revealing."

"I think Gib's seen all you'll be revealing," Sierra had reminded her.

The color in Chloe's face had grown to approximate that in the dress. "Well, everyone else hasn't! And that's all the more reason—"

"I can let it out a little. Really. Look. Just *look*." Sierra had spun her towards the mirror and held her there, forcing Chloe to look at her reflection. "It's not really too tight even now. It isn't snug, it just hugs. And it's stunning. It really is."

"I don't—"

"You have a good eye," Sierra had insisted. "Use it. Don't say no just because it isn't something you're used to. Be daring. Live a little."

"I shouldn't—"

"Alana would."

Chloe did not want to think that Sierra's reminder about what Alana would wear had anything to do with her finally agreeing to wear the red dress. She'd told herself that Sierra was right—it did flatter her figure. Its simple lines seemed to pull the eye to the curve of her hips and the lift of her breasts. And when Sierra had promised to let it out a little, so she didn't feel quite so "revealed," well, how could she say no then?

She couldn't.

She didn't.

But she worried. And now, looking at herself in the mirror, she felt something akin to panic. Sierra had volunteered not only to alter the dress, but to come over early this evening and do Chloe's hair.

"I'm doing Izzy's in the afternoon," she'd said.

"Izzy?"

"Dizzy Izzy, I call her sometimes." Sierra had grinned. "Finn MacCauley's wife." At Chloe's continued blank look, she'd explained, "He's another photographer. Gib and Finn are always going head to head over the good jobs. They're both terrific at what they do. Finn's wife, Izzy, is a trooper. She came to New York two years ago to bring him his nieces and he shanghaied her into staying and taking care of them. Now they're married and they have the girls still and a little boy of their own. Plus Izzy's p.g. again. She's about out to here." Sierra had measured at least half a foot in front of her own slender waistline. "Hard to imagine Finn as a family man, but he seems to have got the hang of it. You'll probably meet them both there."

"That would be nice," Chloe had said politely.

Sierra laughed. "It will be," she'd assured her. "You'll be glad of reinforcements. I'll be there at six to do your hair."

Chloe had had lots of second and third thoughts between then and when Sierra showed up again at six on Saturday evening. "I don't know if I should go," she said when Sierra bounded up the steps and into the living room.

"What? Of course you're going! Sit down in front of that mirror."

"But—"

"Sit," Sierra commanded. "I don't want to hear another word. We've got the dress. You'll have the hair. And you have to go. How else can you tell Dave all about it when you call home?''

''Dave won't care.''

''He'll wonder why you came at all if you turn down opportunities like this one.''

That was, unfortunately, true. Chloe sucked in a deep breath and let it out slowly. Sierra put her hands on Chloe's shoulders and pushed her gently into the chair. Then she began to work.

Chloe had never been able to do much with her hair. It was naturally wavy, and seemed to have a mind of its own. But Sierra was equal to the task. She curled and combed. She teased and fluffed. She pulled a band that was studded with what looked like diamonds from her bag and threaded Chloe's hair through it.

''Oh, my,'' Sierra said as she let her hair cascade around her ears in loose ringlets, then shaped them with her hands. ''Ye-e-s. Ver-r-y sexy.'' She made a noise somewhere between a purr and a growl. ''Let's see how Gibson likes that!''

''He won't even notice,'' Chloe assured her.

''Wanna bet?'' Sierra grinned.

It was a good thing Chloe wasn't a betting woman.

Half an hour later Gibson stood in the doorway staring at her as if he'd been poleaxed. His mouth opened, then shut again firmly.

Chloe looked at him worriedly. ''Are you all right?''

He cleared his throat. He shook his head. His eyes narrowed and he looked at her again. Hard. ''F-fine.'' He ran his tongue over his lips and said it again, just as raggedly as the first time. ''Fine.''

Then, ''Am *I*?'' she asked him, worried again that, despite what Sierra thought, she might not be dressed appropriately. It was to be a Hawaiian night, Gib had told her, whatever that meant. In Collierville it would have implied paper leis and colorful parasols in the drinks.

Gib gulped. "You look...amazing."

Chloe blushed. "It's too tight, isn't it?"

"No!" He cleared his throat again. "I mean, no. It's not at all. It's...spectacular." He let out a sharp breath. "I'll have to beat them off."

Chloe shook her head, flustered. "Don't be silly. It's just...not what I usually wear."

"No kidding."

"I can change."

"You cannot," Sierra said, coming up behind her. "It's perfect, isn't it, Gib?" she said, admiring the dress.

"Very, um, nice. Where'd you get it?" He asked Sierra because there was no doubt in anyone's mind that Chloe hadn't come up with a dress like this one.

"Delia," Chloe said. "Humberto gave it to her after Paris. Thought it was perfect for her. Obviously he never saw it on Chloe."

"No."

Chloe wasn't sure what that meant. It didn't sound like disapproval, but he still looked a little dazed and a trifle green around the gills.

He also, she noted, looked very nice. Not precisely Hawaiian, but very attractive indeed.

Normally Gib wore soft faded jeans and white shirts, half-buttoned, with the sleeves rolled up and the tails hanging out. Tonight he was dressed completely in black. Black jeans. Black boots. Black open-necked, casual linen shirt with the long sleeves rolled back.

For just a second, as she caught a glimpse of her own red dress next to his black ensemble, Chloe thought they might be mistaken for pieces of one of those life-size checkers sets. It made her giggle.

"Something funny?" Gib asked.

"N-no." She smothered the giggle and swallowed the smile, then wetted her lips nervously. "Just thinking."

Gib looked as if he didn't think much of that idea. "Ready?" he asked her.

Chloe looked at Sierra. "Am I?"

Sierra laughed. "Oh, yes. Ooh, yes!"

Gib jerked his head. "Come on, then. We'll grab a taxi."

Chloe opened her mouth to say she was perfectly comfortable taking the subway now, but thought Gib wouldn't appreciate the comment, so she kept her mouth shut. Clutching the small woven handbag Sierra had lent her, she started down the stairs.

The door to Rhys's apartment opened. "Hey, Chlo-o-o-o—" Her name seemed to go on and on as he stared at her in the same poleaxed amazement that Gib had. "Whoa," he said at last. A grin tipped the corner of his mouth. "Dy-na-mite."

Chloe heard Gib's teeth come together with a snap. He took her arm and steered her right past Rhys, so that she barely got to give him a smile. "Excuse us. We're late," he said as he herded her right out the door.

"I thought you said it didn't start until nine," Chloe said as he was tucking her into the taxi.

Gib grunted. He didn't deign to reply.

Neither of them spoke all the way downtown. Chloe didn't know what to say that wouldn't make him regret bringing her. And who knew what Gib was thinking? He stared resolutely out the window, not speaking at all until he told the driver where to stop.

Chloe wasn't sure what she'd been expecting, but it wasn't to get out of the cab in the middle of what looked like a row of six- and eight-story buildings that looked like nothing more than warehouses. She wondered if Gib had got the right address. But he paid the taxi driver and beckoned her out, so she got out after him.

As the taxi sped away, someone opened one of the big heavy doors in the building behind them. A man wearing a

pair of white jeans and a loud Hawaiian shirt held it open
as Gib took Chloe's arm and escorted her in.

The hallway was dark, lit only with two overhead bulbs.
Beneath their feet Chloe could feel chipped black and white
asphalt tile. Very serviceable. Very old. Not very clean.

When Gib had said, "Party," she'd thought of the sort
of parties her parents had—a group of friends who came
over to visit and play cards and share a meal. She'd expected an apartment, not a warehouse. And when Gib
opened the heavy metal door of the freight elevator, she got
downright nervous.

"Are you sure—?" she murmured.

"After you." He held out a hand to encourage her to get
in.

"But—"

An amused smile played around the edges of Gib's
mouth. She wondered if, perhaps, he was having her on, if
he was just testing her to see if she would really believe
there was a party in a place like this, if she was that much
of a hick...

She was just about to say, No way, when the outside door
opened again and half a dozen people, the women in vibrant
dresses, the men in casual slacks and loud Hawaiian shirts,
came in.

"Hold the elevator!" one of the men called.

Gib held it.

Chloe was glad she'd held her tongue. She edged toward
the back of the elevator, letting them all get on. Then Gib
shut the door and one of the other men pushed the button
for the top floor, and up they went.

The elevator rumbled, creaked and rattled its way up. As
it rose, Chloe could hear faint music behind the creaks and
clanks and the chatter of the other women. And then the
elevator shuddered to a stop and one of the other men hauled
back the lever that opened the door.

And as the rest exited, Chloe looked beyond them—

At Hawaii.

Of course she'd never actually *been* to Hawaii, but she'd seen pictures. She'd recognize Diamond Head anywhere. And that was Diamond Head in the distance beyond the small combo—the steel guitar, the drummer, the ukulele, the regular guitar—now playing music that she remembered from when her grandmother used to play albums by Don Ho.

It wasn't just Diamond Head, though. It was the sand. She'd taken a freight elevator to the beach! Her jaw dropped.

Gib grinned. "Come on."

Chloe took a deep breath and followed him. A waiter, clad only in a pair of baggy flower-printed trunks, offered her a drink. It had a rainbow-colored parasol—and a purple swizzle stick in the shape of a long-necked tropical bird.

"What is it?" she asked warily as he handed it to her.

"A mai-tai." He grinned. "A beautiful drink for a beautiful lady."

Chloe looked worriedly at Gib. He arched his brows as if wondering how she was going to react—daring her to behave like the country girl she was.

What did she care if he approved? Chloe thought a little recklessly. *He* wasn't her fiancé!

No, her saner self reminded her. But he was the man who'd brought her here this evening. She didn't want to do anything to embarrass him.

She was counting on him telling her if she was making mistakes. But the look on his face gave her no clue.

She glanced around. Everyone else seemed to be drinking something—or slurping brightly colored slushes that reminded her of the sno-cones she and Dave used to get at the pool in Collierville when they were in junior high.

She seriously doubted they were as innocent as they looked. She might be far better off with the drink, which at least, pretty as it was, looked as though it might be lethal.

As long as she took it slow, she figured she would be all right. "Thank you," she said to the waiter and lifted the glass to her lips.

It was cool and fruity and delicious. And with the press of people growing by the minute, Chloe thought it would be all too tempting to just gulp it down to cool off, then reach for another. She didn't gulp.

She smiled at Gib. He smiled back. Sort of. He looked a little worried.

Determinedly she widened her smile. "It's wonderful," she told him brightly. "The best I've ever had."

The *only* one she'd ever had. But Gib was never going to know that!

"Take it easy," he cautioned.

Chloe nodded, only a little annoyed at his patronizing tone. "Don't worry about me," she said gaily. "This is wonderful!" She gestured with her drink, intending to take in the whole astonishing room. She almost spilled it on a lady passing by. "Oops! Sorry."

"I'll get you something to eat," Gib said. "Don't put too much of that on an empty stomach."

Chloe shook her head. "I won't."

"Stay put," he commanded. "I'll be back."

She nodded. "I'll stay right here."

He looked nervous, though, as if she might vanish if he left her. She fluttered her fingers at him. "I'm fine," she said. She twirled her parasol. "Go on."

She saw his jaw work for a moment, but then he nodded and turned and pushed his way toward where she occasionally caught a glimpse of huge chafing dishes full of what she imagined were hors d'oeuvres. Once he was swallowed up by the crowd, she turned her attention once more to the amazing room.

She could see now that Diamond Head was part of a painted backdrop that hung behind the four men still playing and singing island favorites while half a dozen couples danced on the sand in front of them. Across the room, on what should have been simply another wall, she could see in the distance surfers catching gigantic waves.

"What on earth—?"

"Wanna catch a big one, honey?" A muscled man in a loud print shirt edged up next to her. When she turned, surprised, he gave her a wink and a leer. He also gave a quick thrust of his hips in case she missed the point.

Chloe clutched her drink tightly. "Thank you, but I'm waiting for someone." Then she gave him one of those well-brought-up-but-dismissive smiles her mother had drummed into her at an early age.

Apparently he got the point. He turned and said the same thing to another girl and got an instantly more favorable reply. Chloe, not wanting to eavesdrop, moved away, edging closer to the surfers. She could see now that they were part of a video and that their ocean was really the wall used as a giant screen.

She stood watching, not talking to anyone, feeling the sea of humanity swirl around her, everyone laughing, chatting, talking, schmoozing. She could see the feverish glitter in some eyes, the wary speculation in others. Everyone who was there had an agenda—of that she was certain.

"Here." Gib was back, thrusting a plate into her hand. He checked the level of her drink, then nodded, satisfied, apparently. He took a bite of a canapé and then said over the noise, "So, what do you think?"

"It's not exactly Collierville!" she shouted back. "There are more nose rings than earrings!"

"Gib! Darling!" A tiny silver-haired woman in a caftan buzzed up and aimed air kisses in Gib's direction, then latched onto his arm. "I'm so glad you came. I was afraid you'd be sulking."

Sulking? Chloe looked at him and saw him manage a tight smile as he looked down at the tiny lady.

"I don't sulk, Marie," he said. "You know that. Business is business."

"Ah, yes, *mon cher*, but you could have knocked me over with a feather when Palinkov said no."

Chloe frowned. Wasn't that the designer they'd been putting together the portfolio for? She looked at Gib.

"But I see you have brought consolation with you." The other woman tittered, looking Chloe up and down, a smile on her face. "And who is this, my dear?"

"My assistant," Gib said gruffly. "Chloe Madsen. Marie Kemmerer."

This was Marie? The mover and shaker? Gib's agent? Their hostess?

"Your assistant?" Marie trilled. "Oh, you joker, you!" She gave Gib a playful shove. "I have seen your girls, Gibson. This one is nothing like them!"

"Nevertheless, that's what she is," Gib said flatly.

"That's exactly what I am, Miss Kemmerer," Chloe said, offering their hostess her hand. "I've heard a lot about you. Thank you for letting Gib bring me along."

Marie Kemmerer waved a dismissive hand. "Gib will do whatever he likes," she said, taking Chloe's hand for a moment. "It's nice to have you here, my dear." Then she turned back to Gib. "You must talk to Palinkov. Let him get to know you. Show there are no hard feelings. Come. He's by the palm tree." She began to haul him away.

"Chloe—"

Marie grabbed a passing hunk with her other hand. "Horton will take good care of Chloe," she said firmly. "Won't you, Horton?"

Horton, a bleach-blond California-style himbo with faded blue eyes and washboard abs, smiled a slow, lazy smile. "You bet your socks I will."

Gib looked doubtful.

Chloe didn't want him to feel as if she was an albatross. After all this was work for him. It was just kind of him to bring her. So she smiled a bright, what-a-wonderful-party smile and waggled her fingers at him. "Have fun."

He scowled, then shrugged. "Have fun yourself," he muttered and turned to follow Marie.

"Want to boogie?" Horton asked.

"Boogie?" Chloe dredged up another smile out of the vast repertoire of her mother's polite-in-company expressions. "What fun," she lied.

She was an adult.

A big girl.

It was not his job to keep an eye on her, cosset her, make sure she didn't feel out of her depth.

Hell, he wanted her to feel out of her depth!

He wanted her gone.

And setting her adrift in Marie's Tribeca version of Hawaii was exactly what he'd had in mind when he'd invited her.

So why was he craning his neck, only half paying attention to important conversations, all the while trying his damnedest to spot a golden-haired woman in a bright red dress?

He made nice with Palinkov, kissed the blighter's wife's hand like the polished cosmopolitan gentleman he pretended to be. Then he assured the designer—through clenched teeth intended to look like a smile—that he would be looking forward to seeing what Finn MacCauley did with the coming season's collection. Then he promptly made his excuses and went to check on Chloe.

She was nowhere to be seen.

He'd heard Morton—or whatever the surfer's name was—ask her to dance. But there was no Chloe dancing. There was no Chloe listening to the music, tapping her foot, sipping on a mai-tai, shifting those hips ever so slightly in that stunning red dress.

"Gib! Been meaning to call you!" It was Steve, one of the agency reps he hadn't seen in a while.

Steve wanted to talk about the last shoot they'd done, wanted to relate funny stories of shoots he'd been on, wanted to talk about the Yankees' season. Two of the women who had modeled on that shoot stopped them both. They teased, they flirted.

Gib smiled. He nodded. He kept turning his head, looking for that red dress, those golden curls.

Nope. Nowhere.

It didn't matter, he assured himself. It was what he wanted—Chloe getting swept up in the moment.

No, you didn't, he corrected himself. *You wanted her to get sucked in over her head.*

Well, yes.

So, why are you looking for her? Do you care about her?
No!

"Gib! Guess who's here! Come with me!" Marie was back, tugging on his arm. "I've brought you an old friend! You'll never guess who I ran into at Dumonts' yesterday." She turned him around and he came face to face with the last woman on earth he had any desire to see.

"Gib, darling," Marie said. "You remember Catherine Neale."

Catherine Neale.

He hadn't seen her, in person at least, for eight years. Maybe ten. She was still as beautiful as ever. Her face was more mature now, but there still weren't any tell-tale lines. Her complexion was flawless. The long sable-colored hair he used to love to run his fingers through was fixed differently, though. She no longer wore it down and loose. Now it was piled on her head in a sophisticated twist. On her it looked good, drawing attention to the elegant length of her neck and only enhancing the classic beauty of her features.

"Gib," she said in that slightly husky voice he remembered so well. She held out her hand to him. "Lovely to see you again. It's been years."

"Yes." He shook hands with her. It was all quite civilized. Very formal. "You're looking well."

She smiled. "You, too."

"Oh, you can do better than that," Marie urged them. "Hasn't she grown up beautifully, Gib? You should be so proud. You're the one who first saw it, who first understood how much she had to offer. You were the first to capture Cat on film."

Catherine nodded. "He gave me my start." She turned a smile on Gib.

"My pleasure," he replied. As smoothly as he could, Gib eased his hand out of hers and stuffed it into the pocket of his jeans.

"I'll just leave the two of you to catch up," Marie said, slipping out from between them. "Yoohoo, Rita!" And she was off after another guest.

Gib expected Catherine to give him a one-for-the-road smile and move away quickly. Instead she looked at him, something that seemed almost like concern in her dark blue eyes. "I never meant to hurt you, Gib." Her voice was breathy, quavering almost. She reached out and laid a hand on his sleeve.

In the distance, while she talked to Rita, Gib could see Marie watching the two of them. What was it he'd said to Chloe about her putting combustible combinations together? He thought his was supposed to be Palinkov. He hadn't been expecting this.

Now he took Catherine's hand off his sleeve and, once more, held it for a brief moment before letting it go. "You didn't," he said pleasantly.

She blinked. "I thought—"

"It's been nice seeing you again. Now, please excuse me, Catherine. I need to find my date."

*   *   *

She'd lost Gib hours ago.

At least it seemed like hours.

Horton had swept her off to "boogie." Everyone else was dancing rather sedately. Horton and she had, too. But at the end he'd flipped her back in one of those Ginger Rogers-Fred Astaire moves that she wasn't good at and was totally unprepared for—and besides showing half the party the color of her underwear, she'd been so flushed she'd had to seek out the ladies' room to splash some cold water on her cheeks and restore her equilibrium.

When she came back out Horton, thankfully, had moved on, and Gib was nowhere to be seen.

Not that she intended to hang on Gibson all night.

Chloe knew he didn't expect that. She definitely knew he didn't want it. It was enough that he'd brought her so she could have "a New York fast-lane experience." What she got out of the experience was up to her.

What she wanted mostly was to get out of the experience herself unscathed. A lot of the New York scene she'd been able to take in her stride. Even the bits that seemed out of her "comfort zone" she'd managed to deal with pretty well.

She wasn't so sure about this.

There were so many purposeful people. So many with agendas she didn't understand or knew nothing about.

It would have helped if she could have stayed with Gib—or with someone who would just let her stand by them and watch.

The first thing she did was move as far away from the dancers as possible. She wasn't about to risk another like the one she'd had with Horton. Happily, Horton had set her drink down before she'd felt the effects. Now she went to the bar and asked the bartender for a club soda with a splash of grenadine.

"Sure thing, babe." He gave her a grin and wink and, moments later, the drink.

Chloe thanked him, then edged along a wall, keeping out of the way of the wheelers-and-dealers.

It wasn't easy in that dress. Even though there were plenty of models clearly there to see and be seen, there were also quite a few people who saw—and were interested in—Chloe.

Men she didn't know—or want to—seemed quite eager to chat her up, boxing her into corners and breathing down her neck.

She did her best to make small talk and to keep them at arm's length. When it was clear that she wasn't a model or a designer or a rep from some big agency or company, they lost interest pretty quickly—except for those few who seemed to think she might like to leave with them and, as one put it, "get it on at my place."

"Thank you, but no," Chloe said, polite to the end. And then she ducked under his arm and headed for the stairs to the rooftop. It might be swelteringly hot out there, but it seemed like a better place to hang out—more real than this pseudo-Hawaii that seemed to invite people to leave their good sense at the door.

There were far fewer people up on the roof. It was hot and humid—and the view of the city all around changed the atmosphere completely.

Chloe preferred it. She breathed deeply, almost relishing the ozone and diesel fumes and car exhaust.

She walked over to the edge, set down her club soda and took a deep, calming breath.

"Hiding out?"

Chloe spun around to see an impish female face grinning at her. The woman was short. She didn't have cheekbones. And she was wearing a Hawaiian print dress so determinedly shapeless that it reminded Chloe of her grandmother's muu muu. Not a model, then.

The impish grin got wider. "Can't fit me in a round hole?

Don't worry about it. I'm a square peg here. I'm Izzy,'' she said and offered Chloe her hand.

"Izzy? As in dizzy?'' she said, then blushed, embarrassed.

But Izzy just laughed. "The very one. You know Sierra.'' It wasn't a question.

But Chloe nodded. "I'm Chloe Madsen. I work for Gibson Walker. Sierra did my hair this evening.''

Izzy nodded. "She mentioned you. Told me about the dress. Very nice, I must say.'' Her gaze skated over Chloe's attire approvingly. "She said to look out for you, that you might need a reinforcement or two.''

"I'm out of my depth,'' Chloe admitted.

"Me, too,'' Izzy said cheerfully. "But Finn needs to do this every once in a while. He's not exactly in his element here, either. But he copes. Tonight was a command performance. He's been meeting with a designer for the first time who just gave him a big job.'' She glanced toward the stairs. "Ah, he must have finished. Here he comes now.''

Chloe turned to see a lean, dark-haired, handsome man at the top of the steps, searching the rooftop intently until he spotted Izzy. Then a grin lit his features and the tension in his shoulders seemed to ease as he came toward them.

"This is my husband, Finn. Finn, this is Chloe Madsen. She works for Gibson.''

Finn's dark brows lifted. "You're one of Gibson's girls?''

"For the moment,'' Chloe said. "I'm only here for the summer. I work with his sister in Collierville.''

Both Finn and Izzy looked a little baffled. "Collierville?''

"Iowa.''

They looked at each other. "Gibson's from Iowa?'' Izzy said. "We didn't know that. Another friend of ours, Josie Fletcher, is from Iowa. She lived in Dubuque.''

"That's only about an hour from us,'' Chloe said.

"We were out there last year,'' Izzy said. "Finn did a shoot at the bed and breakfast Josie and Sam were running.''

She and Finn seemed perfectly happy to talk about their stay in Iowa, their good friends Sam and Josie Fletcher, who were now living in New York City, but who went back to Dubuque several times a year.

"We loved it there," Izzy said. "I'd go back in a minute."

"Good fishing," Finn agreed. "Think we might get a place out there, too. It was a great place to kick back and relax once we got rid of the models." He grinned.

"The girls liked it," Izzy said. She told Chloe about their nieces, Pansy and Tansy. When Chloe blinked at the names, Finn shrugged.

"My sister was given to flights of fancy. They're pretty level-headed kids, though. They've had to be with names like that."

The conversation was easy after that. They were curious about the town Chloe came from. She talked about Collierville and Izzy said again how surprised they were that Gib was from there.

"You didn't know?" she asked her husband.

"Gib and I don't chat," Finn said.

"Well, he and I have on occasion," Izzy said. "But I don't remember him mentioning it. Of course, he never talks about anything much that's personal."

"You'd have his life history if you could," Finn said. "Izzy is nosey."

"Izzy likes people," his wife corrected him.

Chloe liked both of them. They were easy to talk to. Finn's dry wit was balanced by Izzy's gentle, good-natured humor. They were the first people she'd met tonight that she felt truly comfortable with.

She asked more about their nieces, then about their year old son.

"His name is Gordon," Izzy said, "after my grandfather who raised me. We call him Rip."

"For a reason," Finn said drily with a grin.

Chloe laughed. The conversation moved easily. Chloe relaxed. Finn got them fresh drinks, then dragged chairs over by the railing so the three of them could sit with their backs to the party and talk. It didn't seem so hot now. A breeze had picked up a little, lifting Chloe's hair, tickling her face. She brushed it away and glanced over her shoulder toward the stairs.

Gib stood there.

He looked the way Finn had—intent, his gaze moving quickly from one group of people to another as he looked for someone.

Who? Chloe couldn't help wondering.

And then he spied her and came straight toward her.

Quickly, with an eagerness that surprised her, she got to her feet. "Gib!"

He seemed to notice just then who she was with and his expression suddenly shuttered. He nodded politely to Izzy, but his lips tightened when he faced Finn. They looked, Chloe thought, rather like gunfighters.

"MacCauley." Gib jerked his head in terse acknowledgment.

"Walker," Finn replied.

"Won't you sit down?" Izzy said brightly into the silence. "Finn can find another chair."

Finn didn't look at all as if he wanted to find another chair, but it was unnecessary in any case. Gib shook his head. "I just came to get Chloe." He took her arm and began to draw her away.

"But—"

"Now," Gib said through his teeth, propelling Chloe toward the stairs even as he did so.

She glanced back and waggled her fingers at Finn and Izzy. "Hope we meet again."

"We will," Izzy promised.

"What's so urgent?" Chloe demanded as Gib hauled her down the stairs.

"You don't need to be consorting with the enemy," he said through gritted teeth.

"*Enemy?* Finn and Izzy MacCauley?"

"Manner of speaking," Gib muttered. "He got my job."

"What job?" Chloe remembered now that Sierra had said something about them competing.

"Palinkov."

Chloe stopped dead. "You didn't get the Palinkov job?"

"No."

She thought he'd explain but he didn't say anymore. She tried to catch his eye, but he wouldn't look at her either. She remembered their argument over what he was going to submit. She'd never actually asked what he had submitted. She didn't think now was the time.

She put her hand on his arm. "I'm sorry."

He shook her off. "I don't need your sympathy."

"You wanted the job."

"Of course I wanted the job! It was a plum!"

"So I'm sorry you didn't get it. I'd like to see what Finn submitted. It must have been amazingly good if it beat yours."

Gib shrugged. "Matter of opinion. Of vision," he corrected, and his mouth twisted.

She touched his arm again, willing him to look at her. And finally, when he did, she said quietly, "You have an incredible vision, Gib."

She hadn't meant it as enticement. She'd only said it because it was true.

She admired his work. She admired his vision. And she wanted—needed—to tell him how much.

She hadn't meant to make him kiss her.

He never meant to kiss her.

Not like that, at least!

Not gently, not tenderly. Not slowly, taking his time to savor full lips and sweet breath. He didn't want to kiss her with hunger, with eagerness, with growing undeniable passion.

Gibson liked kisses.

He never again wanted kisses that mattered.

Chloe's mattered.

To her. He could see it in her eyes when at last they stepped apart and she looked at him, stunned.

To him. He could feel it deep inside. The ice cracking. The heat building. The pain starting. He couldn't do it!

He wouldn't!

He cleared his throat raggedly. "I think it's time I took you home."

CHAPTER SEVEN

HE TOOK her home.

They sat on opposite ends of the back seat of the taxi all the way. Gib stared out the window, fingers clenched into fists on the tops of his thighs. Whatever he was thinking, Chloe was sure it wasn't good.

She, hands knotted in her lap, heart knotted in her throat, tried hard not to think at all.

There was no traffic to speak of all the way uptown. Still it seemed to take a hundred years. For once Chloe had no interest in looking outside, in relishing the bright lights of the city. She was sunk in the black night of her soul.

The taxi barely came to a stop in front of Mariah's apartment when Chloe was wrenching open the door and clambering out. Gib, damn him, climbed right out after her.

"I'm fine," she said, not looking at him, hurrying instead to put her key in the lock. "You don't need to come up with me."

"It's the least I can do."

And that flat statement was worse than anything else he might have said. *It was the least he could do—so he did it.*

She fumbled with the key. He took it out of her fingers and deftly opened the door, then handed the key back. Chloe turned and said stiffly, "Thank you for a nice evening." She hoped he would take it as a dismissal.

He didn't. He held the door. "I'm seeing you all the way up."

She was going to protest, then didn't. It would only make a bad situation worse. She gave a jerky nod and preceded him up the steps as quickly as she could go. The door to Mariah's apartment was easier to open than the front door to the building, thank heavens. And thank heavens, too, that Sierra, who had stayed to let in a plumber, had already gone home.

Chloe couldn't imagine having to talk to anyone tonight. She got Mariah's door open without having to relinquish the key. Then she turned to face him again.

"Thank you," she said firmly. She knew it would be polite to look up and smile at him. But Chloe was beyond smiles. She could manage only so much hypocrisy in one evening.

"Goodnight," she said raggedly. And she shut the door without looking at him at all.

Then, leaning against it and listening gratefully to his footsteps going back down the stairs, she drew a breath—a shaky inhalation that was more sob than anything else. She wrapped her arms across her breasts and just stood and shivered.

She wasn't even sure why. Wasn't sure what she regretted most—kissing Gibson or the fact that he obviously wished he hadn't kissed her.

Everything was a muddle—a mess—her mind, her heart, her *life!*

"That's what you get for playing out of your league," she told herself thickly. "It's what you get for not being satisfied with what you've been given."

She stumbled away from the door and padded into the kitchen. The plumber had, in fact, been there. Both water faucets now worked again. Chloe splashed cold water on her face. Then she stripped off the dress right there in the middle of the room, took the jeweled band out of her hair and ducked her head under the tap. Icy water sent a shock right down her spine.

"It's good for you," she said aloud as if she could cope better if she spoke her thoughts rather than just let them bang around inside her brain. Then she groped for a towel and scrubbed at her hair, at her face—getting rid of the makeup she hardly ever wore, getting rid of the taste of Gibson's lips on hers—getting herself back to reality.

That was when she noticed the note from Sierra on the table.

Picking it up, she read: "Dave called. He is so-o-o nice. Call him. Tell him about the party!"

Yes, Chloe thought, letting the note flutter back to the table. Dave was nice. And kind. And much more solid and sensible than she was. She wanted to call him right then and cry on his shoulder. She wanted to tell him she'd been a fool, that she'd made a mistake, that she was coming home on the next plane.

But she couldn't.

Dave was a dairy farmer. He got up every morning at four-thirty. He would have been asleep for hours, and she had no right to wake him, no right to disturb his well-earned rest just because she'd been a fool and wanted to unburden herself to him.

She couldn't unburden herself to him in any case. There was no way on earth she could tell him what had happened tonight. No way she could explain what she didn't understand herself—why she felt pierced to the heart by the experience of kissing—and being kissed by—Gibson Walker.

The mind was a wonderful thing.

Versatile. Flexible. Capable of uncanny deftness when it came to rationalization.

That was what Gibson thought anyway—because by the next afternoon, he had already managed to come up with a pretty well-developed reason for having kissed Chloe Madsen.

It had been in her best interests that he do so.

It took him a while to work around to that. His mind didn't stop working on it all night.

He'd walked home from having taken her back to her place. He'd figured the night air would clear his head.

It hadn't. Perhaps if the temperature had ever dropped below seventy or the humidity below ninety percent, it would have. As it was, he'd felt as if he was walking home in a steam bath—and in a daze.

All he could think about was the taste of Chloe's lips, their soft yielding under the urgent press of his own, the way they had parted and allowed him entrance, given him the chance to touch her teeth, her tongue.

A shudder went all the way through him.

It made him ache—head to toe. Made him want her every time he thought about it.

What the hell had possessed him?

What the hell had possessed *her*? he thought angrily. She was the one who was engaged, for heaven's sake! She had no business kissing another man!

And she *had* kissed him.

He might have started it. He might have dipped his head, touched her lips—because—hell—she was looking all delectable and delicious, not to mention downright beautiful! But she could have pressed her lips together. She could have sealed them off. She could have made it as enticing as kissing his grandmother.

But she hadn't.

She had melted under his touch. She'd opened to him like a thirsty flower in a soft spring rain. She'd *wanted* to be kissed, damn it!

She'd wanted more than kissing.

And so had he.

And that was what scared the living daylights out of him!

Gibson Walker didn't make love to girls who didn't know the score. He only dallied with savvy women who dallied with him in return. There was no angst, no pain, no heartbreak.

He knew better.

So he should have known better than to kiss Chloe Madsen.

He *had* known better.

He was trying to make a point.

That had been his intention in taking her in the first place. His mind latched onto that, grabbed the notion and clung for all it was worth. Kissing her had just been a part of the whole scheme of things—making her see how risky staying in New York was, staying around *him* was!

He'd kissed her to wake her up, to scare her, to send her back to Farmer Dave in Iowa where she belonged.

Uh-huh.

As long as he didn't look at it too closely, as long as he spent all day Sunday watching tennis on television and was careful to let his answering machine screen calls from his sister and anyone else who might make him probe deeper, he managed to believe it.

In fact, by Monday morning when he set off to work, he had convinced himself that there was a good chance that Chloe might already have left. She might be back in Iowa this very minute!

She was sitting at Edith's desk when he opened the studio door.

She jumped in the chair when he came in, then focused on the scheduling sheet in front of her.

"You're here early," he said. It sounded accusing. He couldn't help it.

She didn't look up. Beyond the fall of wavy blonde hair he could see that her face was pale. He could see, too, that she'd tried to camouflage it by using too much blusher.

He said so. "And it's too red besides. You look like you got in your mother's makeup."

Chloe looked up at him then. She had too much lipstick on, too. He could see that when her overly red lips trembled.

She lurched to her feet and ran toward the bathroom.

"It's not a big deal," Gib yelled after her. "You don't have to start bawling."

The only answer was the slam of the bathroom door.

Chloe had done some stupid things in her life. After this summer she didn't have enough fingers and toes to count them anymore.

But the stupidest—the absolutely dumbest—thing she'd *ever* done was burst into tears just now!

She'd had thirty-three hours to come to terms with what had happened between her and Gib Saturday night. She'd had thirty-three hours to get over that kiss. She should have put it behind her. It hadn't meant anything to him.

It didn't mean anything to her!

Not really.

It had just been unexpected, a shock. And she'd never really been kissed by anyone besides Dave. She simply hadn't known how to handle it.

But she was a grown-up. She ought to be able to get past it.

She *could* get past it—if only she'd stop sniveling every time Gib looked at her!

She scrubbed her face and stared at her blotchy cheeks in the mirror. They were now redder than her lips had been. What an idiot she'd been, slapping on the lipstick like that! As if it would somehow work as a shield to protect her.

Nothing would protect her but acting like the adult she supposedly was.

You've got this far, she reminded herself. Though she'd walked around the apartment hollow-eyed and nauseated almost all Sunday, after a sleepless night, she hadn't given in to the temptation to call Dave or to run home.

In fact, when her mother called to badger her about the wedding invitations and to tell her how irresponsible she was being by remaining in New York, she'd surprised herself by vehemently defending her decision to come.

"You wouldn't want me to be like Dave's sister, would you?" she'd asked, wondering, even as she did so, just where *that* had come from. "She and Kevin got married without thinking—and five years later she was back on her parents' doorstep—with three kids!''

''You'd never do that!'' her mother had exclaimed.

''No, I wouldn't,'' Chloe had agreed firmly. ''And coming to New York is my way of making sure of that.''

There had been a second's hesitation. Then her mother said, ''Are you having second thoughts, Chloe?''

''No! Of course not!''

She wasn't. Her *mind* wasn't.

But last night her body—her emotions—had betrayed her.

Last night, kissing Gib, she hadn't even thought of Dave. Not until Gib had pulled away—and he had been the one who'd broken off the kiss, looking as stunned and anguished as she'd suddenly felt.

Was she having second thoughts?

She didn't know what she was having.

She just knew that going home right now would be foreclosing on whatever was going on. It would be forcing herself to a decision she wasn't ready to make.

Was this the sort of temptation that Sister Carmela had talked about?

Was her restlessness more than just the need to see skyscrapers and museums? Was Gibson her temptation?

And if she resisted—*when* she resisted—would her commitment to Dave be that much greater?

Yes, she decided. That was it.

The kiss had been a temptation. A test.

And like Sister Carmela, she would be strong. She would resist.

She *had* resisted. It had only been a kiss, after all. She hadn't let things get out of hand.

Looked at that way, she'd already triumphed.

Well, maybe she wasn't that good a liar. But she could build on it. She could march right back out there and smile at Gibson and pretend it hadn't bothered her at all.

She could. Yes.

And she would. Right now.

He wasn't in the reception area when she came out. He was already in the studio setting up the first shoot of the day. He was, she could see, doing the things she ought to be doing, doing her job.

She went to help.

Gib brushed her off. "I can manage."

But Chloe shook her head determinedly and reached for the camera he was loading. "It's my job."

He relinquished the camera and turned away.

"Gib?"

He turned his head.

She kept her gaze focused on the camera. "I'm sorry about…that. I don't usually get so…emotional. It was…the wrong time of the month."

She didn't know if he believed her or not. *She* would believe her, if she were told something like that. After all, what other reason could there be for an adult woman to burst into tears when a man said she was wearing too much makeup?

He looked at her a long moment, and she tried to meet his gaze. It wasn't easy, but finally he nodded, as if he was convinced.

"I shouldn't have said what I did," he muttered.

"You were right."

"No, I—" He rubbed a hand against the back of his neck. "It wasn't you," he mumbled. "Didn't look like you, I mean."

"I know." She ventured a faint smile. "Do I look…more like me now?"

"Yeah."

Some tentative rapprochement seemed to settle between them. One thread of communication had been strung.

Chloe breathed a tiny bit easier. She turned to finish loading the film in the camera.

"You...you want to have lunch? Later?" Gib's offer was hesitant. And shocking.

"Thank you, but I'm going to meet Rhys," she said politely.

It was only the truth. But even if it hadn't been, she knew she'd have had to make something up. Gib was a temptation. One she'd resisted.

But there was a limit to her resistance.

She wasn't sure it included lunch.

So she could go out with Rhys. She could make room for him in her work day, for heaven's sake! But she couldn't be bothered with her boss!

Well, who cared?

Not Gib.

Definitely not Gib. He'd only offered because he'd felt like such a louse when she'd burst into tears over the damned lipstick business. How was he supposed to know she was so sensitive?

That was the trouble with women. They were so volatile. So moody.

It wasn't like he *wanted* to have lunch with her! He only thought it might make her happy.

He kicked a reflector out of the way and scowled at the door she'd gone out of half an hour before, hurrying so she wouldn't keep Rhys waiting.

"I'll be back by one," she'd called over her shoulder.

"Take your blinking time," Gib had muttered. "Take all day. Take the rest of your life. Don't come back at all!"

But of course she didn't hear any of it. The door had already shut.

Gib jammed his hands into his pockets and kicked his way around the studio.

"Women!" he grumbled. "Who needs them?"

He felt like banging his head against the wall.

* * *

Rhys had a proposition for her.

"I'm leaving again the first week in August," he told her. "Back to work. And I know you've only got Mariah's place until the end of July. So I thought maybe you'd like to have mine for the last couple of weeks before you go home."

Chloe stared across the table at him, astonished. "Rhys, I…I… Why, that's so nice of you! I hadn't really thought about it."

There had been too much else to think about in her life. In some subliminal way she recognized that every day Mariah's apartment was getting closer to being habitable by someone who cared whether there was hot and cold running water and plaster on the walls.

And she had always known, of course, that after the first of August, Mariah would be back.

But she hadn't thought about where she would go then. Mariah had said they could work something out because it was only a couple of weeks until Chloe would be leaving.

Rhys shrugged. "It was just a thought."

Chloe smiled at him. "A very nice thought. You've been so kind to me, Rhys."

He looked a little embarrassed. "It isn't difficult. You're a far easier neighbor than Mariah," he said wryly.

Chloe blinked. He hadn't even mentioned Mariah until now. She cocked her head. "Meaning?"

"Nothing." He concentrated on the sandwich the waitress had just put in front of him.

Nothing? She slanted him another glance, but he didn't look up. Chloe debated asking a question or two, then decided she'd better not. She had enough problems of her own without getting into whatever was or wasn't happening between Rhys and Mariah.

"I'll give it some thought," she promised. "It's really tempting."

"Well, just know you're welcome," Rhys told her. "Always."

Chloe smiled at him and wished once more that all her relationships with the opposite sex were as uncomplicated as this one.

If Gibson had been like Rhys, the summer would have been smooth sailing.

"Life," she remembered Sister Carmela saying in the interview, "isn't always easy. It wouldn't be interesting if it was. Everybody needs a few white caps, a little wind, to shake things up."

Was that what Gibson was? A white cap?

A tsunami, more like.

"What the hell do you mean, you're moving in with *Rhys*? What happened to *Dave*? Isn't that What's-His-Name's name, for God's sake?"

"My fiancé is Dave," Chloe said calmly, just as if she was making perfect sense. "And I didn't say I was moving in *with* Rhys. I said I was moving into his apartment."

"Excuse me if I fail to grasp the distinction. *His* apartment implies that he lives there."

"Yes, but—"

"And he hasn't moved out?"

"No, but—"

"Then it's damned well *moving in with*!" he yelled at her. "I don't see what else you could call it!"

Chloe sighed. "He's going on duty again. He's leaving next Wednesday."

"Wednesday. And you're supposedly moving when?"

"Well, Saturday. That's when Mariah is coming back. And she's bringing some friends and—"

"Which makes *five days* you'd be *living with Rhys*!"

"Um," Chloe said. She looked a little uneasy. "It's a big apartment," she said after a moment.

"Not that big." Gib was damned well sure of that.

"Rhys is not interested in me."

"Has he got a pulse?" Gib asked. "Then he's interested in you."

"I'm—"

"If you say the word 'engaged' one more time, I'm going to fire you," Gib said through his teeth.

"I was going to say I'm not interested in him." Chloe folded her hands primly and gazed at him like some blinking nun.

Gib snorted. How did she know that? Had she kissed him, too?

He didn't ask. He didn't want to know. He spent the rest of the day muttering and fuming.

He barked at her to hurry up when she was already hurrying as fast as she could. He started to send her home early because he didn't want to see her anymore, then he kept her late because he didn't want her going home and hanging around Rhys Wolfe.

He wanted to kick ol' Dave and tell him to get his butt to New York and watch over his fiancée for himself. It wasn't Gib's job—that was for sure! But somehow, some way, he just seemed to keep doing it!

He needed a vacation. Bad.

He hadn't had one in years. Couldn't remember, in fact, ever having taken one. Not a real, honest-to-goodness two weeks' R&R where he went away from the city and did something entirely different.

What if he did?

It would solve a whole lot of problems. It would keep him well away from Chloe, for one thing. It would keep her from moving in with Wolfe for another. If he left, he could lend her *his* apartment for the last two weeks of her stay.

And when he came back she would be long gone. For good. Forever.

Why hadn't he thought of it before?

*   *   *

"Forget Wolfe," Gib said briskly when he walked into the studio the next morning. "You can move into my place."

Chloe almost dropped the reflector she was moving. "What?"

She was used to Gib striding in and making pronouncements. But this one stopped her cold—and turned her hot—all at once. For one thing it was absurd. For another, it wasn't an invitation. It was a command. She stared at him.

"You heard me. And don't look like I've just made an indecent proposal. I won't be there. I'm going on vacation."

"Vacation? What do you mean, vacation?"

And why hadn't he said something before? She looked from Gib to Sierra who was just coming in behind him. She looked equally astonished.

Gib looked impatient. "You know what vacation is. R&R. Rest. Respite. Repose. Relaxation. The American working man's right to two weeks of hammocks and beaches and basic indolence."

But still Chloe was doubtful. "Now?"

"Now." Gib was firm. "Starting Saturday. *This* Saturday. For two weeks."

"Where are you going?" Sierra asked him.

"Hiking."

"Hiking?" She and Sierra made a duet. They looked at him. They looked at each other.

"You don't know how to hike," Sierra said.

Gib looked offended. "I know how to walk. Hiking is walking without sidewalks."

"If you say so," Chloe said slowly.

"I say so," Gib replied, then turned and walked into the darkroom.

"What's going on?" Sierra asked her when Gib had gone.

Chloe shook her head. "I don't know. He never said anything about a vacation before."

"I didn't even know he knew the word." Sierra rolled her eyes. "Although it's not a bad idea. He's been pretty grouchy lately."

"Missing Alana," Chloe said. She wasn't quite sure what made her say it—or why saying it made her feel all hollow inside. Or why she felt even worse when Sierra agreed with her.

"You might be right. They were getting it on pretty strong before she left. And she's out there somewhere, isn't she? Out in the west? Doing a shoot. I wonder where Gib's going?"

He was going to Montana, he told Chloe later. He'd made a plane reservation for Saturday afternoon.

She could move in that morning, and he would give her instructions, show her where she would be sleeping, what needed taking care of. "You can water the plants," he told her. "Take in the mail. And the morning paper."

It was all very cut-and-dried. He never once asked if she'd already agreed to move into Rhys's. He just assumed she would change her plans to accommodate him.

She wanted to tell him to go jump in the lake—or the Hudson, which was closer. But she couldn't.

If he wanted her to move in, how could she say no? She owed him for having hired her this summer.

As much as she managed was to say, "I really don't need to stay if you're leaving. I mean, who would I be working for if you're gone?"

"You'd be working for me," he said flatly, as if she was stupid not to comprehend the situation. "I won't be home, so you'll be taking care of my place. Rent-free, I might add—and getting to spend the rest of the summer you'd planned on. Unless—" and here he leveled her with an accusing stare "—you intend to walk out on me."

"No. No. Of course not. I'll be there."

And so she was.

Late Saturday morning, she bundled up all her belongings, and Rhys flagged down a taxi, and the two of them moved everything to Gib's place.

"What the hell is he doing here?" Gib demanded when the elevator doors opened and Rhys followed her out, carrying her bags and wanting to know where he should put them.

"He's helping me move in," she said. "Where should he put them?"

Gib pointed down the hall to the bedroom, then turned to glower at Chloe. "I could have helped you. You said he was leaving."

"On Wednesday. So, what do you want me to do?"

Gib scowled in the direction of the bedroom where he'd sent Rhys, then jerked his head toward the deck. "Come on, I'll show you."

First he showed her the bedroom where she'd be sleeping. It had a view toward the park, but what caught her eye was not the sight out the window, but the row of pictures on the wall. They were black and white photos of children playing. Laughing, joyous.

Enchanted, Chloe moved to look more closely.

"Come on," Gib said. "I'll show you what to do with the plants."

Reluctantly Chloe left the photos. She'd have time to study them later. She didn't doubt Gib had taken them, but they were like none of the work he did now. The closest thing she could compare them to, on one brief glance, was the intimacy of the Catherine Neale photos.

"Chloe!" Gib was standing at the door to the deck.

She hurried to catch up with him. She'd never been in an apartment like Gib's. It was huge. Palatial rooms with huge windows overlooked Central Park, and the dining area had sliding doors that opened onto a deck. On the deck, she was amazed to note, there were actually trees and shrubs in over-sized pots. It was amazing.

"If it rains a lot," Gib said, "you won't have to bother.

If it doesn't, there's a hose over there. Use it every other day.'' He showed her how the locks worked, explained the security system, told her the names of the doormen and the superintendent.

''They'll help if you have any problems.''

''It sounds like they could do a better job of looking after the place than I would,'' Chloe said frankly.

''I want someone living here.''

''I wouldn't argue with him,'' Rhys said cheerfully, coming to join them on the deck. ''Nice place you've got here,'' he said.

''Thank you,'' Gib said shortly. ''Don't let us keep you. I want to show Chloe how to work the trash compactor. You don't need to wait around,'' he said over his shoulder to Rhys.

''Oh, I'll wait,'' Rhys grinned. ''We're off to the botanical gardens.''

At his words, Gib went very still. A muscle in his jaw ticked. His fingers curled into fists, and then, carefully, deliberately he uncurled them again. He looked at Chloe for a long moment, his gaze unreadable. If she was going to venture a wild guess, she would have said he almost looked hurt.

But then he said, ''Right. Fine.'' And suddenly he was in a hurry to leave. ''You can figure out the trash compactor,'' he told her, striding away down the hall and grabbing his own bags from what Chloe surmised was his bedroom.

He handed her two keys and headed for the door. ''The smaller one is for the mailbox. It's in the lobby. Mail comes about two. Thanks. Goodbye, Chloe Madsen. It's been…interesting.''

And before Chloe realized she was probably never going to see him again, Gib was out the door, into the elevator, and gone.

She stood there, staring after him, bereft, hollow, until

Rhys came up behind her. "Hey," he said, "how about we go get a meal?"

It had been the right thing to do.

The only thing to do. And it was going to be fine, he assured himself as he settled into his seat on the plane and pulled the baseball cap down over his eyes.

He had someone taking care of his place. He was doing a good deed for his sister's friend, allowing her to stay in New York and at the same time attempting to protect her from unscrupulous wolves.

It wasn't his fault if she was stupid enough to accompany one to the botanical gardens! He had done the best he could.

Now he was going to enjoy himself. He was going to kick back and relax, forget about everything that mattered, focus on mountain streams and clear running rivers, on bears and deer and fish and other assorted sundry wildlife. He was going to breathe deeply the fresh alpine air and relish the expanse of Montana wilderness he hiked through.

He was on vacation.

He wasn't going to give another thought to New York, to his business, to Chloe Madsen. Not at all.

He shoved it all out of his mind as the plane hurtled down the runway. He closed his eyes and settled back to think vacation thoughts.

Tonight would she sleep in his bed?

CHAPTER EIGHT

CHLOE didn't sleep in Gib's bed.

She did, however, wander through his bedroom more often than was probably good for her.

Of course, because she didn't have to go to the studio anymore, she was free to do whatever she wanted in New York City for the next two weeks—she could play sightseer every day if she wanted to.

And occasionally she did. She went to all the places she'd missed: the Cloisters, to the Museum of the American Indian, to the Guggenheim and the New-York Historical Society, to the Museum of American Folk Art and the Museo del Barrio and the Cooper-Hewitt and the Museum of the City of New York.

She knew she couldn't go home without seeing and appreciating them all.

But mostly she stayed in Gib's apartment and appreciated Gib.

She'd been immediately impressed by the huge rooms with airy views across the park. But more than the rooms and more than the views, what impressed her were the photos on the walls.

And what they told her about Gib.

She'd expected photos of his work. She'd anticipated seeing blow-ups of the best of his "less-is-more" shots of the world's most beautiful women.

There were blow-ups, all right. But very few beautiful women. At least they weren't beautiful in the classic sense that the women he photographed daily were beauties. And they weren't all women, either.

The photos were mostly of people, that was true. But they

136

were as often of children or old people as they were of young adults in their prime. Few of them were set obviously in New York. To Chloe's surprise, a lot of them seemed to have been set in Collierville. She recognized some of the settings—which were cluttered and busy—not stark like his later work. He'd caught people in the midst of what mattered. She began to recognize some of the people, too.

There was one photo, hanging above the table in Gib's kitchen, of old Mrs. Hellier who had died a few years ago. In this picture she looked a good fifteen years younger. Her back had been straight, as she'd stood hanging out sheets in a snapping breeze. It was a glorious picture. Every morning Chloe stood and looked at it and felt the wind herself, remembered Mrs. Hellier's stubborn independence, her strength, her brisk no-nonsense ways. It was all there in the picture.

She recognized the children in the photos in her bedroom as young brothers she had occasionally babysat for. They were sledding down Bunker Hill, shrieking with that childish combination of terror and glee, emotions she identified with now, and remembered feeling every time she'd hurtled down the steep, fast slope.

In all the photos she saw the same intensity that Gibson brought to work every day. But she saw more. She saw involvement. She saw caring, compassion, concern. She saw the sort of emotional connection between artist and subject that she didn't find in his commercial work. She hadn't seen it in any of Gibson's work since the Catherine Neale book.

But it was here. And because it was here, she knew that once it had mattered to him. The more she saw, the more she wanted to know why he'd changed.

And the less she wanted to think about him at all.

The girl who sold him his fishing license had golden curls. Nice. But they didn't glint warmly in the sun. Not like some he knew. This girl's curls didn't make Gib want to reach out and touch them. They didn't smell of flowers and sunshine. They weren't really the same at all—not even close to the glory that was Chloe's hair.

The thoughts skipped through his mind with such amazing swiftness that they'd come and made their mark and gone before he could resist them.

He didn't *want* to think about Chloe Madsen. He'd gone half a continent to get away from her.

She was with him every step he took.

The way her curls warmed in sunlight, the way her lips curved in a delighted smile. The way her hips swayed when she walked across a room. The way her breasts jiggled when she reached up for something on one of the shelves.

They were the standard against whom all the women he saw were now measured. Other women's hair wasn't as wavy or as golden. No one else's lips had quite that full a curve. Other hips were too wide or too narrow. Other breasts had absolutely no appeal.

Chloe's did. Still.

Damn it.

The first day, of course, when all these "Chloe thoughts" flitted through his head, he thought it was just the residual effect of having spent so much time in her company. Naturally he would remember her hips, her breasts, her lips. They were the ones he saw every day.

He didn't stop to think that he saw many other women's lips, hips, and breasts at least as much. His models, for example. They were work. Sierra. He couldn't remember Sierra even having breasts. He supposed she must.

He only remembered Chloe's.

He tried to forget. But walking around Bozeman didn't help. Every time he saw a girl with golden hair, every time a pair of hips sashayed along the sidewalk in front of him, he was reminded again.

He went back to the motel room he'd rented for the night

and turned on the television. He watched mindless garbage that wouldn't distract a five-year-old. It certainly didn't distract Gibson.

He discovered that the pay-per-view movies he could get would only make him hornier. He didn't bother. He got up and took a long cold shower instead.

Tomorrow, he promised himself, things would be better. Tomorrow he would be so busy hiking and taking in beautiful scenery that he wouldn't have time to think about Chloe Madsen at all.

Tomorrow, he discovered, when it finally rolled around, was no better than the day before.

In fact, it was worse.

Gibson took his rental car and drove up into the mountains. They were every bit as lovely as he'd hoped. It didn't take long to leave civilization behind. He rattled up the narrow dirt road to the trail head that he'd marked on the topographic map he'd bought at the sporting goods store. There he parked the car and locked it, then shouldered the backpack with attached bivy sack and set off toward the ridge.

He had a map. He'd bought a book that practically outlined every step of the way he'd decided to go. He was healthy, fit, and determined. How hard could it be?

Hard.

Very.

He'd forgotten about the altitude. He wasn't used to it. He got winded a lot more quickly than he imagined. He'd forgotten he hadn't broken in his new hiking boots. Hell, when had he had time to break them in? It wasn't as if he'd been planning this trip for a long time. It was definitely a spur of the moment venture. He'd forgotten that in Montana, even in summer, it could snow.

Snow?

He didn't believe it when those first few flakes drifted down. He was more inclined to believe the old children's story about God shaking out the feather pillows than he was to accept the fact that it was actually snowing.

It didn't take him long to become a believer.

The temperature dropped. The wind picked up. The snow began in earnest. Gib turned and headed back down.

He hadn't packed for snow. He was a fair-weather hiker at best, a fair-weather camper barely.

Snow?

In a word, no.

So he ended up back at the motel, damp and shivering, with blisters on his heels and time on his hands. More garbage on television. And once again the temptation of those pay-per-view blue movies.

And he *was* tempted because, through it all, the one thing he hadn't forgotten all day was Chloe.

At first it had been, *Chloe would think that's a fantastic view.* Then it had been, *Chloe would like to see a flower like this,* or *I wonder if Chloe has ever been camping?*

And then it had been, *Chloe wouldn't believe this. Snow! In July!* Then, *Would Chloe cringe if it started snowing on her?* And finally, *This is insane. I've got to go back. I just won't tell her.*

It wasn't until he was back, taking a hot shower this time, that he remembered that he wasn't ever going to see Chloe again.

Somehow it wasn't as comforting as he'd hoped.

He lay on the bed and conjured her up, smiling at him, then batting her lashes at him, then wiggling her hips and pursing her lips.

He groaned.

Then he did what he'd sworn he wouldn't do. He got up and dug through his backpack and pulled out the pictures he'd stuck down at the bottom beneath his socks. The pictures of Chloe he'd taken that first day. Chloe, naked and alluring. And some other Chloe photos, too. Ones he'd snapped at the end of a roll "to finish things off," he'd assured himself. She wasn't naked in those. She was sometimes pensive, sometimes laughing, sometimes thoughtful. But always alluring, too.

He shouldn't have brought them. He couldn't remember why he had.

Well, yes, he could.

He remembered thinking that he'd pull them out and look at them every few days, just to test himself, to see how far he'd come in his resisting-Chloe-Madsen campaign.

The theory had been that as his resistence grew he would be able to look with indifference at the photos for an increasing amount of time.

Judging from his present reaction, he had a hell of a long way to go.

That was probably why he was a little over-eager to get back into the mountains as soon as the snow had melted in town.

"Not sure you ought to be hikin' up there right now," the desk clerk at the motel told him when he checked out. "Pretty slick still. Snow might be gone down here, but it'll linger for a while up high."

But the forecast looked good for the next few days, and Gib needed distraction. Badly. "I'll survive."

Three days later, thinking about Chloe instead of where he was going, he slipped. He fell.

He broke his leg.

He survived. Just.

Less than twenty-four hours and she'd be home.

Chloe sat on Gibson's bed and tried to think herself back to Iowa, tried to imagine getting off the plane tomorrow evening and being crushed in Dave's welcoming arms.

Her bags were packed. Gib's plants were watered. Everything was neat and clean, ready and waiting for him. She'd even baked some cookies and left them on the counter for a thank-you in case she missed him, though she couldn't help hoping she'd hear from him before she left for home.

She hoped he would call just so she could tell him how much she'd appreciated the chance to stay in his wonderful apartment, just to thank him again for letting her be his assistant for the summer, just to say goodbye.

To hear his voice one more time.

The thought jolted her. She almost jumped off the bed. She shouldn't have been sitting on it in the first place. Now she hurriedly straightened the coverlet so he'd never know.

And then she sat down again.

Couldn't seem to help herself.

"Thank you," she said softly to the room, where she'd come sometimes late at night to read, to sit, to ponder, to think.

She knew she shouldn't. She had a bedroom of her own. She had the whole apartment to read in or to sit and think.

But no place was as comfortable as this. Oddly, there were none of Gib's photos in here. Just three framed snapshots sat on top of the dresser—of Gina as a young woman, of Gina and her husband and children, and of a happy young couple she suspected had been Gib's parents.

The man had Gib's dark hair and intense gaze. The woman had his quick smile. They were standing outside Rasmussen's Ice Cream parlor in Collierville. Chloe had recognized the setting at once. She'd smiled when she'd seen it, had felt a familiar warmth and longing for home.

That was probably why she came in here. Because she felt closer to home.

And because she felt closer to Gib?

She shoved the thought firmly away.

She was going home.

Tomorrow she would be there. Her New York interlude would be over. Her life—the life she'd planned since she was eighteen years old would be squarely in front of her again.

She tried to imagine it. Tried to think how she would get off the plane, and Dave would be there to meet her. She would run to him and he would put his arms around her. She would hold him close, too, and know that this was where she belonged, that, like Sister Carmela, she had come home and all would be right with the world.

She lay back on the bed now and drew one of Gib's feather pillows into her arms. She hugged it close against her chest, pressed her face into its softness and breathed deeply as if it were already tomorrow, as if this were Dave she was holding.

But it wasn't Dave. Not yet.

Tonight she was in New York. And she knew she would remember this moment forever. This room. This bed. This pillow. She drew a breath and knew she would remember it, too.

The smell of the city. The smell of soft cotton.

The indefinable scent of Gib.

The ringing phone startled her.

Chloe, jolted awake, forgot for a moment where she was, then realized she'd fallen asleep on Gib's bed. Scrambling up, she glanced at the clock. It was late. After eleven.

She picked up the phone. "Hello?"

"Did I wake you up?"

"Gib!" She couldn't keep the pleasure out of her voice, didn't even try. He *had* called to say goodbye! "How are you? Did you have fun? What did you do?"

"Broke my leg."

"What?"

She didn't think she'd heard right. His reply was so laconic, so flat. So completely Gib. "When? How? Are you all right?"

"I'll live. I just need you to do me a favor."

"Anything." She jumped off the bed, fluffed the pillow,

smoothed the coverlet again, as if he could see where she was.

"Call this number and have them send a car to the airport for me. I'll be in at two tomorrow afternoon. I'd take a taxi, but it's easier this way." He rattled off the number and Chloe quickly wrote it down.

"I'll call right now. But—"

"Thanks." He hung up before she could say another word.

With the dial tone buzzing in her ear, Chloe stood staring at the phone, astonished.

So much for saying goodbye.

Well, Chloe resolved, it wasn't going to be goodbye. Not yet. Not if he was hurt.

She felt that odd lingering sadness that had plagued her all day as she'd packed begin to lift slightly. She picked up the phone and called home.

"I can't come tomorrow," she said without preamble.

Dave wasn't happy. Her mother wasn't happy. There were flowers to be chosen. A menu to be picked out. Two hundred wedding invitations demanding to be addressed.

"Later," Chloe said and, when she hung up, felt immeasurably lighter.

Poor Gib had broken his leg.

"What the hell are you doing here?" Gib stared at Chloe, appalled.

He'd had an awful flight. His ankle, in a non-walking cast for two more weeks, was still aching and swollen seven full days after surgery and three days after he'd been released from the hospital.

He could have gone back to New York then, but he hadn't. He'd stayed in Bozeman until the day he was supposed to fly home—had got himself a place with room service, and had holed up there, counting the days until Chloe was gone.

And now, damned if she wasn't waiting at the gate as he crutched his way off the plane!

She looked briefly stricken at the sight of him, then hurried forward, a sustaining smile on her face. "Oh, Gib!"

He didn't feel sustained. He held himself rigid. If she threw her arms around him, he didn't know what he'd do. A man only had so much will-power. Gib had used most of his. He felt beleaguered, harassed, not at his best. He didn't want to have to act like an adult. And he certainly didn't want Chloe there!

He fended her off with a crutch. "I thought your plane left this morning." He tried to maneuver his way around her.

It was futile, of course. She didn't touch him, but she fell into step alongside him, moving a little ahead actually, as if she were some damn fullback running a down field block for him.

"It did. I wasn't on it. The driver is waiting by the baggage area." Her hips were swaying ahead of him. He closed his eyes, almost stumbled over the damn crutches, cursed.

She stopped abruptly and steadied him. "Are you okay?"

He tried to shake her off. "Fine, damn it! Why aren't you in Iowa? You're supposed to be in Iowa." It was possible that he sounded petulant. He didn't care.

She started walking again, slowly, so she wouldn't outdistance him. "I was. I'm not. I told them I wasn't coming."

"You what!"

She looked back at him, blonde curls bouncing. "I couldn't leave you."

He expected her to look immediately abashed at how he might choose to take that declaration, but she didn't even seem to notice.

"I didn't want you to be alone," she went on.

"I'm all right!"

"You need help."

"I don't!"

"Yes," she said patiently, as if explaining things to a particularly dim child, "you do. So I'm staying on."

Staying on? Had she said, *staying on?* He stopped dead. Chloe kept walking.

"Hey!" he yelled after her. "Hey! What do you mean? You're not staying on!"

She stopped. She came back. She smiled at him. It was the last thing he needed—a Chloe Madsen smile.

He resisted. Mightily.

"Of course I am. Try and stop me," she said cheerfully.

Sometimes, in Gib's adolescent fantasies, he had been the brave soldier, fighting for right, defending honor, being injured in the process, and finding solace, devotion and unstinting care in the arms of a beautiful girl.

Gibson Walker: wounded hero.

Reality didn't measure up.

If there was honor in falling over a log and crashing down a hillside, Gib supposed it had been in trying to keep away from the all-too-enticing, but completely unsuitable and unavailable Chloe Madsen.

But even if you stretched honor that far, he still couldn't take solace in the arms of the woman displaying her care and devotion because, damn it, the woman was Chloe!

And for all that she seemed determined to be devoted and unstinting in her care of him—bringing him food and magazines and books and unending good cheer, tucking in his blankets and propping his ankle up and fluffing his pillows, all the while quite inadvertently touching him as she straightened the bedclothes, brushed his hair off his forehead, handed him silverware—she was every bit as unsuitable and unavailable as she'd ever been.

She was driving him crazy.

He wanted to make love to her.

It wasn't fair!

Gib had gone through nearly a dozen years being pretty

much immune to women. He hadn't been celibate the entire time, but he'd never felt a stirring of interest in one particular woman. He'd simply taken them as they came, had charmed them and dallied with them, but had never really cared about one more than another.

Catherine had taught him well. After Catherine he'd never let any get close.

He wouldn't let Chloe get close.

But still he wanted to make love to her.

He'd tried to fight it every way he knew how. It hadn't done any good. He wanted her more than he ever had. And he wasn't going to get any respite from her now. She was in his apartment, fussing with his bedclothes, fluffing his pillows.

Now she took away his dinner tray and smiled at him.

He shut his eyes, resisting. "How's Dave?" he made himself ask.

The smile faded briefly. Then, as if she realized it, she pasted it back on again. "He's fine," she said briskly. She bent and straightened the damn blankets once more. As she did, she touched his arm, his leg. Lightly. Not even noticing.

He noticed.

One feather's worth of touch and his whole body seemed to respond, to tighten, to vibrate with a need for her. She moved down to adjust the pillows under his ankle. She bent her head. He wanted to reach out and thread his fingers through her curls. He wanted to pull her to him, to draw her down upon him and slide his hands up under her shirt.

He wanted to touch those wonderful jiggly breasts. He wanted to nuzzle them, to kiss them, to suckle them.

He groaned.

"Oh, heavens! Did I hurt you?" Chloe jumped back away from the pillows, looking at him stricken.

Gib, taut with need, with hunger, with unrequited lust, couldn't even answer. Could barely swallow.

At his silence she looked even more worried. "I'm so

sorry, Gib.'' She was fussing with the blankets again, pulling them down now. ''You can't be comfortable like that. You should have got in pajamas hours ago. Let me help you.'' She reached for the buttons of his shirt.

He yelled, ''No!''

''But—''

He waved his hands at her, shooing her away, feeling like an idiot when, damn it, he should have been allowed to feel noble. ''Just no, for God's sake! Don't you speak English?''

She backed away, but she didn't leave. ''Well, you can't sleep in your clothes,'' she said, and she sounded like nothing so much as the mother of a stubborn five-year-old.

Gib shifted irritably on the bed. ''I wasn't planning to sleep in my clothes.''

''Then tell me where your pajamas are and I'll get them for you.''

''I don't have pajamas,'' he said through his teeth.

''What?'' She didn't look as if she'd heard him right.

''I don't wear blinking pajamas,'' he shouted at her. ''I sleep nude!''

''Oh.'' It wasn't a word, it was a squeak. Color flooded Chloe Madsen's face. Her gaze dropped from his face to the middle of him, then jerked right back again. ''Oh,'' she said again, and blinked rapidly several times. ''Of course. Well, um, I'll just take this tray and leave you to it, then.'' She backed toward the door. ''If you need anything, just, um, call.''

She fled, banging the door shut behind her.

Gib settled back against the pillows and let out a soft, frustrated moan. God, was he noble or was he noble?

Gina would have told him to look for the silver lining. He tried.

All he could come up with was that at least now something else besides his ankle hurt.

CHAPTER NINE

IT WASN'T the thought of Gibson naked that did it—though the thought was certainly compelling, God knew. The notion had tantalized her for weeks. She'd lain awake some nights just thinking about it—about *him*. And, she supposed, she should have realized something was wrong just from her fixation on that.

But she hadn't, because she hadn't been thinking straight.

She'd thought that all she needed was a little time and a little space and all her qualms, all her restlessness would be settled. She'd thought that, like Sister Carmela, she would test the temptations of the big wide world and come back to Dave, committed, confirmed, at peace.

She was wrong.

She'd succumbed.

Not to the world.

To Gibson.

She had known the truth of it when she'd watched him hobble off the plane this afternoon.

His face had been drawn with pain, his features etched with exhaustion. She thought he'd lost weight. His knuckles had been white on the crutches. He'd seemed barely able to stand up.

And she'd never seen anyone look more wonderful in her life. She'd felt a surge of joy so powerful, a leap of longing so intense that it almost knocked her to her knees.

It was the way she'd imagined she would feel when she went home, the way she'd expected to feel when she got off the plane and ran to meet Dave.

She knew now, in a moment of blinding clarity, that it would never happen.

149

She had never felt—would never feel—like this about Dave.

She loved him—had for years.

But not the way she loved Gibson Walker.

There was no denying it any longer.

She'd wanted to run to him right then, to throw her arms around him and hold him close, to tell him she'd missed him, that she'd lived every day inspired by the photos he'd taken, that she could hardly wait for him to come home.

In fact she'd *started* to run toward him—and then she'd seen the look of panic, of desperation that had flickered across his face.

It had stopped her dead. It had made her pause and regroup, then face reality.

Reality demanded that she approach him more slowly, smiling and friendly. Detached but determined. She was, after all, Chloe-the-assistant.

"Gibson's girl," she whispered in a raw, aching voice now as she huddled in her bed.

That was how he saw her. That was all he wanted from her.

She would never be Gibson's woman because, for all that she loved him, she knew he didn't love her in return.

The next morning she called Dave.

She didn't know how to tell him. She wondered if she should wait until she got home so she could say it in person, then knew she couldn't.

Already she'd waited too long.

There was nothing to do but tell him straight out. "I can't go through with it," she blurted when he answered the phone.

"What?" Of course he wasn't expecting to hear from her at the crack of dawn, but she'd wanted to reach him before he went out into the fields for the day. Besides she'd lain awake most of the night worrying—and trying not to hear Gib tossing and turning as well.

"The wedding," she tried to explain now. "I can't marry you. You know my...restlessness? Well, it's not...gone."

"What do you mean? You said...you were sure..." Dave groped for words, then stopped. She knew he was baffled—and hurt. He had every right to be. She didn't blame him. Only herself.

"It's my fault," she said. "Nothing to do with you. Just me."

And the way I feel about Gib. But she didn't say that. It would be cruel.

"It's just 'out of sight, out of mind.'" Dave argued with her. "It's because I'm not there, because you're not here!"

"No."

But Dave wasn't convinced.

"We were too young when we decided to get married," Chloe told him. "We were children."

"We were in love."

"Yes, *were.* But now..." The words died. She couldn't say them.

Dave said them for her. "But now you're not." She heard the pain in his voice, felt like a heel, like pond scum, like the lowest thing since dirt. And yet she knew that going home and marrying him would be wrong, even if she didn't love Gib.

It wasn't as if she was going to marry him! It was that he'd shown her how much more deeply she could feel—*should* feel—before she made a lifetime commitment.

"I do love you, Dave," Chloe protested faintly. "But not..." She felt tears welling. "Oh, God, I'm sorry! I don't mean to hurt you."

He didn't say anything. She had no right to expect him to, of course—no right to hope that he would forgive her, would tell her she wasn't hurting him.

"I'm sorry," she whispered again.

"We can work it out, Chloe."

But she didn't let him finish. "No," she whispered, "we can't."

She hung up and pressed her palms against her face, hating herself for having hurt him.

She didn't suppose it would be much consolation to Dave to know that, in loving Gibson unrequitedly, she would be hurting, too.

She didn't take off her ring.

She didn't tell Gib what she'd done.

If she told him she'd called the wedding off, he would want to know why. Worse, he would already have guessed.

She could just imagine what he would think then. Poor pitiful Chloe couldn't even love the man who loved her. She had to be a fool and fall in love with the man who never would.

An involuntary shudder ran through her. Maybe she was a coward, but there were some things that, in the interests of self-preservation, were better left unsaid.

So she tried to smile and behave as she always did. Dutiful, helpful Chloe. Smiling and talking. Fetching and carrying.

And all the while she did so, she made memories. Because she knew that even though she wasn't going home to marry Dave, she would have to leave sometime.

And when she did, memories would be the only things she would have.

He tried once more on Sunday to tell her she didn't need to stay.

He punctuated his diatribe by poking the air with his crutch—a sort of physical exclamation point—which would have been a lot more convincing if he hadn't lost his balance and practically fallen over as a result.

He would have fallen on his face if Chloe had not dodged

the crutch and grabbed him, hauling him upright and, incidentally, into her arms.

His own went right around her to steady himself. And the feel of her soft, yielding breasts beneath the hard press of his chest sent a surge of longing shuddering right through him.

Chloe seemed to tremble, too, for a moment. They stood, pressed together, hearts thumping wildly. And then, carefully she stepped back, putting space between them, steadying him only with the grip of her hands on his upper arms.

He didn't need the support now. He had his crutches back on the ground. He was solid, steady now—on a physical level. He dropped his head forward, stared at his feet, and tried to regain his mental equilibrium.

"I'm staying," Chloe said into the silence broken only by the harsh sound of his breathing.

He lifted his head and gave it a rueful shake. "I figured you might."

Maybe that was the point at which he gave up the fight.

A man only had so much will power. Gibson had run through his. He'd tried. For *weeks* he'd tried to resist her.

He didn't have it in him to combat her attraction any longer.

What was more, he didn't want to. He was tired of being noble, sick of pretending he didn't care.

If she was going to be fool enough to stay, to fuss over him, to touch and pat and brush him—if she was going to play with fire—well, so be it.

"Do you want to go out on the deck and sit in the sun for a while?" she asked him now a little warily.

He raised his head and looked at her. God, she was beautiful—heart and soul and mind, as well as body.

He wanted her.

Now...and forever.

The thought shocked him. Jolted him right down to his toes. He hadn't thought in terms of forever since Catherine.

Surely he wasn't...

Yes, he was.

She's engaged, he reminded himself. *She's going to marry Farmer Dave.*

Oh, no, she wasn't.

Not if Gib could stop her.

They went out on the deck.

It was a bright clear sunny day with low humidity, the kind of Sunday that only comes once a year and which New Yorkers who spend weekends in the country regret having left the city for.

Chloe led the way, still trembling a little from their encounter in the bedroom. She'd expected him to push her away after she'd steadied him. She'd been surprised—and she'd stayed in his embrace too long—when he hadn't.

After she'd stepped back, she'd shot him a quick glance, expecting to see a derisive curve to his mouth. But his head had been bowed. He was breathing heavily and his knuckles were white against the hand grips of the crutches.

She'd almost reached out to touch him again. Only sanity and self-preservation had prevented her.

And then he'd said in an oddly subdued voice, "Yeah, let's go out on the deck."

Now she pulled out a pair of redwood chaises longues and folded mattresses out on top of them, then laid a pair of brightly patterned beach towels on those. Gib hobbled out after her and dropped down onto one of them.

"Can I bring you anything?" she asked him. "Something to drink? One of the books? A magazine?"

"How about my camera?"

She blinked, startled, then nodded. "Where is it? In your luggage?"

"The black case. The small one."

She hurried off to the bedroom and came back with it moments later. Gib had stripped off his shirt and lay there wearing only a pair of cut-offs and his plaster cast. She wished she'd brought her own camera out.

This would be a memory worth preserving.

"Thanks." He took the case from her and opened it, took out his camera and fitted on a lens. Then he pointed it at her.

Chloe jumped away. "Gib! Don't!"

But he didn't pay any attention. He clicked away, smiling at her.

"Gib!" She protested again.

He lowered the camera, still smiling. "I don't have enough pictures of you," he told her. "You're beautiful."

The way he looked at her when he said it made Chloe swallow hard. She shook her head quickly. "Don't be silly. And don't tease."

Gib's mouth tipped at one corner. "I'm not teasing, Chloe." His voice was soft and a little husky. Sensual.

Chloe made a face at him.

He grinned. "Nice." He raised the camera again and recorded it for posterity.

"Stop!"

"I will when you do."

"What's that mean?"

He reached out and patted the other chaise. "Stop bustling around. Come sit by me and relax."

Chloe sat down. She even stretched out. She didn't relax. How could she possibly when just inches away Gib was stretched out, too?

She shut her eyes and turned her head away from him. But knowing he was there made her want to look. She shifted her body, angled her head the other way, allowing herself a peek at him from beneath her lashes.

He winked at her.

"Gib!"

He laughed. "Caught you!"

"I was only concerned," she said haughtily. "I don't

want to hover, but I do want to be aware when you need somethin~ Do you need anything?''

"You."

The world seemed to stop.

Chloe stared at him.

Gib stared back. He didn't blink, he didn't smile, he didn't shake his head and say he didn't mean it. Instead he reached out a finger and ran it lightly down the length of her forearm.

Chloe trembled. *No. Oh, no!* She couldn't!

Could she?

Something in her face must have betrayed her panic.

Gib smiled ruefully. "Want to use the hot tub?"

"Wh-what?"

He pushed himself up against the back of the chaise and tipped his head in the direction of a large, covered object against the kitchen wall. "I just thought you might like to use the hot tub. It doesn't take that long to fill. It's a nice day…" His voice trailed off. He cocked his head, looking at her.

Chloe was still stuck on the *you*. Still trying to come to grips with…with *what*? But she couldn't ask. And she wouldn't make him repeat it!

"I…I'd like that."

She'd never been in a hot tub before. They weren't thick on the ground in Collierville. But even if she'd enjoyed them daily, she'd have said yes now because it would get her up and moving, giving her something to do.

"I'm sorry I can't fill it," Gib said. "But it's not very hard."

Chloe hadn't even bothered to look at it while she'd been here alone. But now she took the cover off it, then ran some water in it, as Gib directed, and rinsed it out before turning on the hot tap all the way and letting it fill.

It was good-sized. Big enough for six, Gib told her. Did he fill it when he had parties up here? Chloe wondered.

Had he shared it with Alana? The thought came to her unbidden—and unappreciated.

"It should be full in about half an hour," Gib said. "Go get your bathing suit on. Unless—" he gave her a teasing grin "—you want to skinny dip?"

"No," Chloe said quickly. "I'll...I'll be right back."

He had plenty of opportunity to call a halt.

At any time during the afternoon he could have retreated into surly irritability. He could have had an attack of scruples and stopped smiling at her, charming her, subtly flirting with her.

But he did not.

Because he wanted her. And he didn't care about the ring on her finger or the man she intended to go back to.

He shot more photos of her when she came back out wearing her bathing suit. She scowled at him, made faces at him and shooing motions with her fingers. But Gib was impervious.

He just smiled and snapped away.

Once she was in the hot tub, he slung the camera strap around his neck and hobbled in closer, coming to perch on the edge of the tub to shoot down at her. He had a wonderful view of the tops of her breasts peeking just above the roiling foam of the water.

Then Chloe looked right up at him and didn't make a face. Her expression softened. Her lips parted.

Gib groaned. He ripped off the camera and set it aside, then leaned toward her and kissed her.

It was like coming home. Warm, welcoming. Everything a kiss ought to be.

And not nearly enough.

Gib wanted more.

He tangled his fingers in her hair and felt hers, warm and wet, come up to touch his shoulders, to grip him tightly, to pull him closer.

He slid sideways, lost his balance. "Oh, hell!"

He went in head first, smashed his face against her breasts, felt her grapple to haul him up and almost protested. It would have been a sweet, sweet death.

But the look on her face, his name on her lips, when she hauled him out—"Gib! Are you all right?"—that was better.

He laughed and shook his head, scattering water everywhere. "Yeah," he told her when he stopped coughing. "Oh, yeah."

"Your cast?"

"Didn't get it in. It's fine. I'm fine. I...want you." He was done playing games, done biding his time, done teasing. He looked at her. Challenged her. Waited.

Slowly she nodded her head.

How could she have said no?

What she wanted, of course, was to love him for all time. What she was going to get was one night.

A stronger woman might have forgone it.

Chloe took the night.

For the memory, she told herself. For the years ahead when she was old and gray and long since alone.

But for the moment, too.

I love you she told him with her eyes. *Forever,* she told him in her heart. *You're perfect,* she said with her hands as they slid up his chest and traced the curve of his neck and the line of his jaw.

"Oh, Gibson," she whispered aloud.

"Come with me?" he whispered back.

She nodded and climbed out of the tub. Carefully he dried her off. The rough yet soft terry of the towel scrubbed lightly across her shoulders, then down over her bathing suit to begin work on her legs. As he rubbed, his damp hair brushed against her and she put out a hand to touch it, to touch him. He lifted his gaze, his eyes dark and slumberous, heavy with desire, and he took her hand and turned it. He pressed a kiss into her palm. Chloe shivered.

Then he stood and she slipped her arm around his waist, not so much to support him as simply to touch him, and together they made their way to his bedroom.

She looked at the rumpled, unmade bed and remembered lying there the night before she'd been going to go home, remembered taking his pillow into her arms and holding it close, thinking that was as close as she would ever get to holding him in her arms.

And now?

Now she stood before him, holding her breath, waiting, anticipating.

Gib faced her, laid his crutches aside, then wobbled on one foot, and had to sit on the bed. He looked up at her and grimaced.

She smiled and touched his rueful mouth with one finger. His lips parted. He touched the tip of her finger with his tongue, laved it. Then he reached up and slipped his fingers under the straps of her bathing suit and slowly, deliberately peeled it down.

Chloe trembled under his touch, shivered at the memory of the last time she'd been naked before him.

This time he leaned forward and touched his lips to each of her breasts in turn. His mouth played with the rosy-tipped peaks, suckled on them, making Chloe quiver and burn.

Her hands came up to fist tightly in his hair. She dropped her head forward, pressed a kiss to the top of his head, then fell forward, as he fell back. And as he rolled back, he peeled her suit the rest of the way down. Chloe came down on top of him, breast to chest, lips to lips, toes to toes.

She felt a shudder run through him. She smiled. She looked into his eyes and saw wonder there. She felt a quickening wonder of her own. His hands smoothed down her back, then locked her tight against him as he lifted his hips, giving her hard evidence of the extent of his arousal.

Chloe tried to sit back, but he held her fast. She reached to touch the waistband of his cut-offs. "Let me..."

He nodded jerkily. His eyes were hooded, pupils dilated, the skin across his cheekbones taut. His breathing was quick and shallow. And it got even quicker when she sat back on his legs and undid his shorts.

He bit his lip as she slid her fingers inside the waistband and eased the zipper down. Then she pulled back and dragged them down his legs and over his cast, then tossed them onto the floor.

At last.

Gibson Walker naked.

A sight well worth waiting for.

"C'mere," he muttered.

And she barely got a chance to appreciate his lean, hard body, his hair-roughened chest, his muscular legs before he snagged her hand and pulled her back on top of him, groaning with pleasure at the way their bodies fit.

Chloe felt her own pleasure, and gave a little wiggle, enjoying the feel of him, hard and hot beneath her. She rubbed her body against his.

Gib's hips bucked. "Careful, sweetheart," he rasped. "I'll be through before we've even begun."

Sweetheart. Chloe hugged the endearment to her heart. Made it a memory. Tucked it away. She touched his cheek. She kissed his eyelids, his nose and, finally his lips, and felt herself swept away by his kisses in turn.

"We'll make it last," she promised him.

He wasn't promising forever. She understood that much. So if this was all she was ever going to have of him, she would make it last and last and last.

He loved her once.

He loved her twice.

He loved her more times and ways than he could count.

He remembered those photos of Chloe naked. He remembered imagining how he would like to touch her, to caress her, to make her respond.

Neither the photos nor his imagination came close to the real thing.

She was perfect. Glowing. Responsive.

She received. She welcomed him. She wrapped her body around him and took him in.

And she didn't only receive. She gave. There was nothing calculated about Chloe. Nothing artificial. She gave him her all—he could feel it—loving him with her body, her mouth, her lips, her hands until it almost felt as if she'd wrung him out.

He lay back, sated, amazed.

She looked down at him. "What?"

He laughed a little raggedly. "I'm just trying to...adjust my thinking."

She cocked her head, a tiny frown line appearing between her eyes. "What do you mean?"

He grinned. "I never thought Collierville High was on the cutting edge of education. But sex ed classes must have taken a quantum leap since I left."

"Oh!" Chloe dug her fingers into his ribs, tickling him, making him grunt and grab her hands, then, careful not to kick her with his cast, he rolled her over and pinned her beneath him.

"My turn," he said hoarsely, slipping between her legs.

"Can you? With your leg, I mean?"

"We'll find out, won't we?" he said. He moved carefully. She eased her legs wider to give him greater access. Then she touched him gently and once more brought him home.

They slept. Then they woke and kissed and snuggled some more. He dared her to teach him more Collierville High moves. She responded with an enthusiasm that both delighted and shocked him.

"I thought you were an innocent," he told her. "Unawakened."

Something flickered in her eyes for just a moment, making him tense. But then she smiled and curled in his arms, putting her head on his chest and pressing a kiss against his breastbone. "I was," she told him. "Completely unawakened. Until I met you."

It must have been the middle of the night by the time she finally fell asleep in his arms.

Gib settled back and cradled her body against him, watching her sleep, tracing the curve of her cheek with his thumb, then twining his fingers in her silken curls. Her lips pursed. She mumbled, then smiled just a little.

Gib bent his head and gave her a kiss.

Then, smiling, he slept, too.

The phone woke them.

Chloe answered it before Gib could tell her not to bother, before he could bury it under a pillow and haul her back into his arms.

"What?" she said. All the color seemed suddenly to drain from her face.

Gib edged up against the headboard of the bed. "What's up?" he asked sleepily.

Chloe wetted parched lips. "Of...of course," she said. Her voice sounded hollow. "S-send him up."

"Somebody bringing us breakfast?" Gib asked lazily. "I don't suppose we have time for a quickie first?" He grinned.

But Chloe was shaking her head, scrambling out of bed. "Dave's here!"

It was the last thing he expected. He stared at her. "What?"

She plucked his cut-offs up off the floor and flung them at him. "You heard me! Get dressed!"

And she flew out of the room to get dressed, too.

Gib had his cut-offs on when the first hard knock sounded on his door. Chloe was still buttoning her shirt as she went to open it.

"I wouldn't—" Gib began.

But she already had.

And Farmer Dave stalked in. He took one look at Gib, another at Chloe and, apparently, saw all he needed to see and knew all he needed to know. His jaw hardened. His face reddened. His fingers curled into fists.

"Dave! Don't!" Chloe began.

But Dave did.

Just one punch. Gib saw it coming. Didn't duck.

He reckoned he deserved it even as it rocked him backwards and he fell.

"Omigod!" Chloe flung herself at him, dabbing at his bleeding lip. "Oh, Gib!" She turned and shot a fierce look at Dave. "How could you?"

"How could I not?" Dave countered. He stood over Gib, breathing hard, a muscle ticking in his jaw.

Gib pushed Chloe away. "Don't," he told her. "I'm all right."

"But—" She looked devastated, caught between the two of them. A position he'd put her in.

"I'm sorry," he said. He looked at her, then at Dave. "I never meant—I didn't want—"

It wasn't true. He had meant… He *did* want…

But one look at Chloe's distraught face and he knew there was no way on earth he could make amends. He had taken her innocence. Deliberately. Determinedly. Selfishly. He'd used her to get what he wanted.

Just like Catherine had once used him.

She reached for him again, but he pushed her away. "I'm all right," he said harshly. "Don't worry about me. I deserved it."

"But—"

"You did," Dave agreed flatly. "Come on, Chloe."

"No, I—"

"Go with him, Chloe." Gib forced the words out of his mouth.

She looked at him, stricken. And then when he stared back at her, her expression changed. It grew remote, resigned. Still, though, she didn't move.

"Go on, Chloe," he said harshly with all the will-power he had left. "Just go."

CHAPTER TEN

IT WAS not the homecoming Chloe had planned.

Her mother was apoplectic. Her father was amazed. Her sisters looked at each other and shook their heads.

"What happened?" everyone asked her.

Chloe wouldn't say. *Couldn't* say. How could she tell them that far from coming home settled and focused, ready to tie the knot, she'd discovered that the love she felt for Dave wasn't enough, that it didn't hold a candle to what she felt for another man?

It would hurt Dave.

It wouldn't help her.

And she couldn't bring herself to talk about the other man.

Not even to Gina who looked at her narrowly when Chloe came back to work. "You're not marrying Dave?" she asked.

"No."

Everyone in Collierville had heard the news within an hour after Chloe and Dave had got back. Two days later when Chloe went into the *Gazette* for the first time, Gina expected an explanation. Chloe didn't offer one.

But Gina wasn't content. "Gibson didn't do anything, did he?" she asked suspiciously.

Chloe shook her head. "No! Of course not."

There was a pause. Then she asked, "He was a gentleman?"

"Always," Chloe said firmly.

Gina sighed. It sounded almost like a sigh of dismay and Chloe, who wasn't expecting that, looked at her strangely.

"I almost wish he had." Gina explained her consternation

165

ruefully. "Done something. Got involved. Smitten. I wish he'd find a nice girl like you and settle down."

Chloe stared.

Gina reddened. "Oh, I don't mean I sent you there so he could break up your engagement, but...I sort of hoped he'd see you and think about marriage again. Once upon a time I thought love and marriage were what he wanted."

Chloe shook her head slowly. "No. I don't think so. Not Gibson."

Gibson was a willing bed partner. Inventive and attentive. Both tender and eager. She'd remember the sweetness and the passion of their lovemaking for the rest of her life. And she'd never be able to pass Collierville High without wondering what they were teaching in the sex ed classes these days.

Because ultimately that was what it had been between her and Gibson—sex ed.

He'd never said, "I love you."

He didn't love her.

Chloe knew he never would.

Chloe and Dave's broken engagement was, in the annals of Collierville history, more than a nine-day wonder. Nothing much happened in Collierville. So it was a good three weeks before something noteworthy enough came along to dislodge it as the principal topic of conversation.

Chloe never thought she'd be personally grateful for a broken latch on the back of a trailer carrying seventy-eight hogs to market. But when the hogs scattered all over the highway and it took seven hours, one truck driver, two fire trucks, seven pickups, nine farmers, three journalists, a photographer and two mayors to round them up, suddenly there was more than the lack of wedding bells in the air.

The escapee hogs were the first to divert attention from Chloe and Dave. And then Chuck Hayes pitched a no-hitter in the annual Collierville semi-pro baseball tournament, and the sheriff's office found a meth lab in the woods near Hobart's farm, and the parish festival was just around the corner, and the pennant race began heating up and it looked like the Cubs might have a chance...

Chloe began to breathe a little easier. She didn't sleep much better, though.

And then as she was leaving work the Friday after Labor Day, she ran into Dave.

It was the first time she'd seen him since he'd left her at her house the day they'd come back from New York.

A dozen times she'd wanted to call him, to try to smooth things out, to apologize all over again.

But she never did. She had no idea what to say.

She didn't have any idea now.

But with Mrs. Timmerman and Mrs. Vogt coming down the street and Leo McCarthy watching from the hardware store window, she knew she couldn't just pass him by without a word.

She didn't want to pass him by in any case. He was still Dave—one of the dearest people she'd ever met. She wanted them to be friends, even if they were never going to be spouses.

She looked at him, made eye contact, ventured a smile. "Hi."

He smiled, too. It was the first time she'd seen him smile since she'd left back in June. The sight gave her a lump in her throat. "How've you been?" he asked.

"All right. And...you?"

"Getting better." He actually sounded better, too. As if he was recovering nicely. As if she hadn't broken his heart.

"I'm glad," she said fervently. "I...wanted to call you. To see," she explained. "To ask. But I..." Her voice trailed off.

Dave smiled wryly. "Better you didn't."

They looked at each other. A long look. As if they were seeing each other clearly for the first time as adults.

"Yes," Chloe said.

There was a moment's silence between them. She wondered if that was the end of it. And then he said, "You were right."

She tipped her head. "Right?"

"About you and me. About...breaking it off."

Her eyes widened slightly. "How did you...why do you...?" But she wasn't even sure what to ask.

"I called your landlady."

Now Chloe's eyes really were wide. "My *landlady*?" What landlady?

"Mariah," Dave said. He shrugged. "I wanted to understand. I needed to know what went on, to figure things out. I wondered if letting you go out there in the first place was a mistake."

"You didn't 'let' me," Chloe informed him stiffly. "You couldn't have stopped me."

Dave nodded. "I realize that. After I talked to Sierra, I realized a lot of things."

"You talked to Sierra?" Chloe blinked.

"Well, Mariah didn't know anything, but she said her sister might. So she gave me her phone number. And I talked to her. She told me..." He paused. There was a sudden increasing hint of redness along his cheekbones. He cleared his throat and began again. "She told me you...danced naked...for Walker."

Chloe gaped. She looked around wildly. Fortunately no one was close enough to hear! "She *told* you? She said—!" Her mouth opened and shut like a fish's.

"She said it was a mistake," Dave told her quickly. "But I thought, That's not Chloe. That's not the Chloe I know. The Chloe I know would never..." He shrugged again. "And the more I thought about it, the more I thought you were right. We've grown up. We got engaged a long time ago, when we were kids—and we never questioned whether it was right for us when we got older. Well, that's not true.

I think you questioned. Didn't you? That's what this was all about, wasn't it?''

He was looking at her intently, openly. Curiously.

And Chloe had to nod, because it was true. "I thought I'd find that we were right for each other," she told him. "I really did. I wasn't trying to break things off."

"I know," Dave said, his voice almost gentle. He hesitated, then rubbed a hand against the back of his neck. "I'm sorry I punched him."

"It wasn't his fault."

"He's a fool."

"No—"

"Yes. If he doesn't love you, he is. A damned fool. I told Sierra so."

"You did?" Chloe was horrified.

Dave nodded with apparent satisfaction. "Sierra agrees with me."

"You discussed it?" Chloe felt a shroud of fatalism descend.

"Mm-hm. She's a nice girl, Sierra is." He smiled again.

There was something about his smile that made Chloe narrow her eyes as she looked at him. Dave and Sierra? It didn't seem likely. It barely even seemed possible. But stranger things had happened.

They certainly stood a better chance of happiness than she did by having fallen in love with Gib.

She cocked her head. "Tell me," she said to Dave. "How do you feel about purple hair?"

Gib felt like hell.

It was understandable. His life was a mess. His priorities scrambled. His long-held resolutions shattered.

"You knew better," he told himself. "You knew she was trouble."

But knowing hadn't made any difference.

He wanted to call up Gina and tell her off. He wanted to

yell at her, tell her she'd had no business sending Chloe to ruin everything, to play havoc with the smooth running mechanism that was his life.

Of course he didn't.

He would never call Gina and say any such thing. He didn't talk to Gina about his personal life. He hadn't given her a chance to comment in years. He sure wasn't going to start with this!

Besides, he'd get over it.

He'd got over Catherine, hadn't he?

No problem. A week. Two, maybe. And then he wouldn't even think about her anymore. He'd barely remember her name. She'd be just another of "Gibson's girls," here one day, gone the next, like Whatever Her Name Was, the one who'd come before her.

Before Chloe.

Chloe.

He could close his eyes and see those blonde curls of hers. He could remember tangling his fingers in them. He remembered her lips, too. The way they kissed. The way they smiled. He remembered the sound of her laughter, the eager enthusiasm with which she approached every day, the gentle warmth of her eyes when she looked at him.

When would he forget her name?

Not for a while, he feared.

He would have had a shot at getting over her if he'd been able to go to work. If Chloe had been there, he would have ignored his broken leg and gone to work anyway. She was quick enough and clever enough—and had her own vision well developed enough—that he could have had her do some of the shooting.

But Chloe was gone.

Edith was still in North Carolina. There was no one to hire the next of his girls. And just as well because Gib couldn't bear thinking about a new one.

He wanted the old one!

He wanted Chloe!

But he couldn't have her. He had what he deserved for trying to take her—a split lip and a guilty conscience.

Chloe belonged to Dave.

He'd done what he had to do—pushing her away, sending her back to Iowa with Dave, being noble.

His sister Gina was very big on nobility. He supposed she'd be proud of him. But only after she raked him over the coals for being an unthinkingly greedy, selfish bastard first. She would be appalled at him for having "taken advantage of" Chloe. Gina thought in expressions like "taken advantage of."

Gib used to scoff and tell her she was old-fashioned, that there was no such thing as "taking advantage of."

"It's tit-for-tat, don't you know?" he remembered saying to her when she'd criticized his cavalier attitude toward having relationships with women. "They use me, I use them."

Gina had just shaken her head and said sadly, "That's not always the way it is, you know."

He knew.

He'd done his best to forget over the years. He'd tried to pretend it didn't matter. And he'd done a pretty good job on himself.

Until now.

He was a heel. A rat. In the overall scheme of things Gib figured that he ranked somewhere lower than whale dung.

He deserved to feel bad—and he felt awful.

Just deserts, he told himself bitterly as he sat on his deck and stared glumly at the hot tub, remembering, aching.

The worst of it all was that, even knowing he deserved to feel rotten, even knowing he had taken what he had no right to take, he still couldn't help being glad he had the memories.

And he still couldn't help wanting Chloe.

The phone rang, shattering his misery. He stared at it. He hadn't answered many calls in the three weeks since Chloe had left. He hadn't wanted to talk to anyone. He didn't want to talk to anyone now. But on the fourth ring, after the answering machine told the caller to leave Gib a message and he'd get right back to them, an irritated female voice said, "Gibson Walker, if you are there you had damned well better answer this phone or find yourself another agent!"

Gib cursed under his breath. He'd been avoiding Marie as well as everyone else. He'd called her once to tell her he'd broken his leg and wouldn't be working. She'd said, "You don't press the shutter with your toes, Gibson."

He'd let her phone messages pile up since. She was right, of course, but he couldn't do it. Not now. Not yet.

"Gibson! Pick up the damn phone!"

He picked up the phone. "What?"

"Ah." She breathed a sigh of satisfaction. "You are there. Does your leg keep you from picking up the phone, too?"

"I picked up the phone, Marie," Gib said through his teeth. "What do you want?"

"I want to make sure you're going to be at the Guerilla Lounge tonight for the *Seven!* party."

Gib didn't answer. He shut his eyes. He tried to think of some reason not to be there. Short of being dead and buried, there wasn't one that was going to convince Marie.

"Gib?" There was a mixture of imperiousness and annoyance in her tone. "This silence had better be acquiescence, not mutiny."

"My leg—"

"You don't have to dance, sweetheart. You simply have to show up and smile politely and receive the accolades that are your due. The ads are stunning. The girls are extraordinary."

Not as stunning or extraordinary as the one he'd left out.

"I'll see you there," Marie said and hung up before he could tell her he wasn't coming.

In the end, he went. He didn't see what else he could do.

He did want to work in this town again. He didn't want to snub the hand that fed him. Besides, he told himself, it would be salutary to get out, to stop moping around, to act as if it was the first day of the rest of his life.

The trouble was, as far as Gib could see, thinking of it as the first day of the rest of his life didn't improve things a whole lot. In fact, from where he stood the rest of his life looked pretty damn awful.

He hoped to breeze in, say a few pleasantries, make sure Marie knew he had come, and then breeze right back out again. But his cast slowed him down, a dozen scantily clad women oohed and cooed over his injury, all of them offered to kiss it and make it better, most of them offered to come back home with him and nurse him back to health, three told him they knew how to take his mind off his pain.

He thought he ought to take at least one of them up on it.

He said, "No," and, "No," and, "No," again.

Finally he felt a hand on his arm and heard a cheerful female voice say, "Stop fussing over him. He's fine." And he turned to see Finn MacCauley's wife shooing them all away. "He just needs to get off his foot for a while so he's coming with Finn and me."

It was perhaps an indication of how desperate he felt that leaving with Finn and Izzy MacCauley sounded preferable to standing there trying to be polite.

"You are ready to go, aren't you?" Izzy favored him with a smile.

Gib nodded.

"Good." She took his arm with one hand and looped her other through Finn's. "We're off, then."

What Finn thought of Izzy bringing Gib with them wasn't immediately clear. But he didn't object when Izzy led the two of them out, waggling her fingers cheerfully at Marie as they left.

It was only when they were on the sidewalk that she

dropped the plastered-on smile and sagged a bit. "There," she said to Finn, "aren't you proud of me? Only ten-thirty and we're free."

He nodded, but he gave Gib a questioning sidelong look as if to say, What's he doing here?

"He looked like he needed rescuing, too," Izzy said in reply to the unasked question. She smiled at Gib.

He drew away and nodded briefly. "Thank you. I appreciate it."

"Oh, for heaven's sake, don't go all stuffy on us now. I know you and Finn compete, but there's nothing around now to take a picture of, so let's just play nice, shall we?"

Gib looked at Finn. Finn looked at Gib. Finally Finn gave a rueful half laugh. "Izzy is a bit of a force," he said.

"A bit?" Izzy gave him an arch look.

Finn grinned. "I'll play nice if he will." He looked once more at Gib who, bemused, found himself nodding.

Izzy beamed at them both. "Come back to our place," she said to Gib.

He knew Finn and Izzy lived on the Upper West Side, too. He didn't realize they lived on the block behind Mariah's place. He could see the apartment where Chloe had lived from the deck off the MacCauleys' living room.

Finn brought him a beer, and Izzy carried in a bowl of chips. They all sat down. Finn said something about the weather. Izzy said something about the children. Gib said nothing at all.

He couldn't. He could only look across the garden and the fence and stare at the bedroom window of the place where Chloe had lived.

"I was sorry to hear Chloe left," Izzy said, as if she were reading his mind.

Gib's head jerked up. "What?"

Izzy smiled. "I liked her. A lot. We had some good times."

"You did?" The words came out almost strangled. Gib

remembered she'd met Chloe at the Hawaiian party. He hadn't thought they'd met again.

But Izzy nodded. "While you were hiking out west and she was sightseeing," Izzy said, "the girls and I went with her sometimes. It was fun. She was fun. I thought you and she..." Her voice trailed off.

Good thing. Gib bent his head, studiously rubbing the condensation off his beer glass. He hoped no answer would get Izzy to change the subject.

He hoped in vain.

"Why did you let her go?"

"Izzy isn't only a force," Finn said casually, "she's also damn nosey."

"I'm concerned," Izzy corrected. She leveled a gaze on Gib. "Why did you let her go?"

"I didn't *let* her go," Gib protested, stung by the accusation. "She was always going to go. She was engaged when she came here! She's getting married the day after tomorrow!" He almost couldn't make himself say the words. His fingers gripped the glass so tightly his knuckles turned white.

"And you're letting her?" Izzy sounded shocked.

Gib stared. "What the hell else am I supposed to do?"

"You could stop her."

Oh, sure.

He was just going to jump on a jet, rush right out to Iowa, then charge into the church yelling, "Stop the wedding!"

Uh-huh. Gib could really see himself doing that.

The trouble was, if he *didn't* do that, Chloe was going to be making the biggest mistake of her life.

And how, after three weeks of certainty that he'd done the *right* thing, was Gib now convinced that he'd done the wrong one?

Because sometime, somehow, some way, he realized that

Chloe could never have made love with him so totally, so purely, so sweetly, if she didn't love him.

To do what she had done with him, she had to love him! So why the hell was she marrying Dave?

Because you threw her back at him, you idiot! he told himself. *In your completely insane, totally misguided fit of nobility, you took her love, then you turned right around and threw her away!*

"Of course you have to stop her," Izzy said "I don't see that you have any other option."

And Finn actually agreed. "Nobility," he'd said somewhat enigmatically, "isn't all it's cracked up to be."

Gib was beginning to get that idea.

When he got home, he yanked open his closet, grabbed out his duffel bag and started to pack.

Collierville.

It was everything he remembered—several hundred houses of clapboard and brick, an equal number of well-tended lawns and colorfully planted flowerbeds, tree-lined streets with children on bicycles zipping to and fro. It was Norman Rockwell's America—or as close as Iowa could come.

He recognized it all, saw it as if he'd left yesterday. It was the first time he'd been back in a dozen years.

Once it had been the home of his heart.

Then he'd denied he had a heart.

And now?

"What goes around comes around," Gib muttered as he stopped his rental car in front of his sister's house and got out. Wasn't that what they said?

God, he hoped so.

He was only halfway up the walk when the front door opened and Gina stood staring at him—at first in amazement, then in delight. "Gib!" she shrieked, and she hurtled down the steps and flung her arms around him, squeezing him in the way that only Gina ever squeezed. "Oh, Gib! At last. You're home! Why didn't you call? Why didn't you say?" She had him by the arm. She was dragging him toward the house. "Why are you—? No! I won't ask! I don't care! I'm just so pleased."

She would care, Gib knew.

She would be furious with him. She would tell him he had no right to step in, no right to interfere, no right to tell Chloe not to go through with it.

"I'm so glad you're here!"

"You won't be when you find out why," Gib told her.

She stopped on the porch. She stepped back. She didn't let go of his arm, but she did step back—far enough to look into his face. "What are you talking about?"

"I came to stop the wedding."

She didn't blink. Not right away. She looked at him, her expression blank. And then she said, "Wedding? What wedding?"

Gib gritted his teeth. "*Chloe's* wedding! To Dave. Who the hell else do you think I'm talking about?"

Gina shook her head. "There isn't going to be a wedding."

Now it was Gib's turn to stare. "What? What do you mean there isn't going to be a wedding?"

Once more Gina shook her head. "They called it off."

He didn't dare hope.

He didn't dare not.

"Why did they call it off?" he demanded.

Had it been Chloe's idea? Or had Dave told her he didn't want her after finding her with Gib?

Gina didn't know whose idea it had been—or why.

"I need to talk to Chloe!" Gib was heading back down the steps now. "Where is she?"

"I don't know," Gina said. "She took some time off. Went away."

"Away? Away where?" For God's sake, wasn't she even in town?

Gina shrugged. "Dave might know."

He was supposed to ask *Dave* where Chloe was? He'd be asking for another split lip. Or maybe a black eye.

A small price to pay, he decided. He needed to find Chloe.

"Where's Dave?"

He found Chloe's ex-fiancé working on a tractor. Dave was no more thrilled to see him than he was to see Dave.

"What do you want?" the other man asked. There was no welcome in his voice.

Gib couldn't blame him. "Not another split lip," he said. "Though I deserved the first one."

"You did," Dave agreed. "What are you after now?"

"I need to find Chloe. My sister said she isn't around. She said you might know where she is."

"I might." Dave went back to fiddling with the wrench.

Gib waited, balancing on his toes, his fingers curling lightly into fists. He understood that he could wait forever as far as Dave was concerned. He would have to ask. "Will you tell me? Please."

Dave met his gaze levelly. "Why should I?"

"Because I love her."

He'd fought it as long as he could. He couldn't fight it anymore. Gibson Walker loved Chloe Madsen. It was the stark, simple truth.

He bent his head. He closed his eyes.

"There's a cabin," Dave said slowly. "Near the monastery. I'm not sure she's there, but I'd be willing to bet."

Chloe wondered why she'd never considered a monastic vocation before.

It was quiet, it was peaceful, it was a whole lot less stressful than her life had recently been.

"Because it's a cop-out if you're using it for a refuge," Sister Carmela told her. "You don't go into the monastery to avoid your problems."

"You don't?" Chloe said. "Oh, darn."

Sister Carmela laughed. "You can't run away from yourself, Chloe."

Chloe smiled wryly. "You mean, wherever you go, there you are?"

"Exactly." Sister Carmela squeezed her hand. "You just have to face yourself—your hopes, your dreams, your blessings, your failings—whatever is in your heart."

That would be Gib, Chloe thought.

Because if wherever she went, there she was, then Gib was there, too. In her days and in her nights. In her hopes and in her dreams. His presence went far beyond the memories she had of him. She was her best self when she was with him. Just like Sister Carmela was her best self in the monastery.

"But he doesn't love me," she protested. They were sitting on the small front porch of the cabin as they did every afternoon. For most of the day Chloe stayed on her own, thinking, walking, coming to terms. And then, in the afternoon, Sister Carmela would come to chat for an hour or so.

"Spiritual direction," she called it.

Chloe said direction wasn't enough; she needed a map.

Now Sister Carmela smiled. "I think you'll see your way before long. And I wouldn't be so sure he doesn't love you. You never know what's on the horizon." She looked beyond Chloe at the top of the wooded hill beyond the cabin. Then she smiled enigmatically.

Chloe smiled back, wishing Sister Carmela wouldn't be quite so cryptic. "My horizons are pretty limited," she replied.

"They might be broader than you think." Sister was still looking past Chloe, still smiling, looking speculatively at Chloe and then beyond her again.

Finally Chloe turned her head. "Gib?" His name was a heartbeat, a stammer, no more.

He was halfway down the hill, in a walking cast now, she saw. At least she hoped it was a walking cast. He wasn't using crutches. He was limping badly and coming so fast he was going to fall on his face if he didn't slow down!

"Gib!" She leapt up to run to him, knocking over her chair as she did so.

She heard Sister Carmela behind her, getting up, too. "I thought it might be," she said.

So much for circumspection.

So much for playing hard to get.

But after Chloe had spent the past few weeks facing every minute the truth that she loved Gib with all her heart, how could she possibly greet him with casual indifference?

She couldn't.

But she probably shouldn't have knocked him down in her enthusiasm, either. "Omigod! I'm sorry!" She'd only meant to throw her arms around him, to intervene in his headlong descent and hold him close.

Well, they were close, all right. She was on top of him.

Gib wasn't complaining. He was tangling his fingers in her hair, kissing her fiercely and, when she would have pulled back, refusing to let her go.

Chloe didn't argue. She was perfectly happy to keep kissing. Out of the corner of her eye she saw Sister Carmela smile and give her a thumbs up, then disappear down the trail toward the creek.

Chloe looked after her for an instant, sent a fleeting prayer of thanksgiving for the woman and her wisdom and, mostly, for her discretion. And then she went back to kissing Gibson again.

It was better than all her memories put together—the feel of his body, hard and solid beneath her own, the rasp of his whisker-roughened cheek against hers, the hot, hungry press of his lips. Oh, yes.

"Why the hell didn't you tell me you'd called the damn wedding off?" he demanded when he finally dragged his mouth off hers long enough to take a breath. He glowered up at her, breathing hard.

She smiled and shook her head, unrepentant now. "Because you'd have thought I was pathetic."

"What!"

She shrugged and sat back, but he didn't let her go far, kept a hand on her wrist like an anchor. No, Chloe corrected herself, like a lifeline.

"It was self-preservation," she explained. "What was I supposed to do? Tell you you'd spoiled it for me and Dave? Admit I couldn't possibly marry him when I felt the way I felt about you? Throw myself on your mercy?"

Gib grinned. "It would have helped!" He pushed himself to a sitting position and then his expression grew serious. "Did I?" he asked her. "Spoil it for you? Are you... sorry?"

And all at once the cocky man she knew looked uncertain. He looked as weary and worried as she'd been the last few weeks. He looked as if his life hung on her answer to the question.

And Chloe reached out a hand and touched his. Her gaze locked with his. "I'm not sorry if you love me, too."

The sound he made was somewhere between a laugh and a sob. "More than I ever imagined loving anyone. I never wanted to love anyone again."

"Again?" It was a question only if he wanted to answer it. She knew all she needed to know now. She knew he loved her.

But he slanted her a glance and nodded heavily. "Catherine."

"Catherine Neale? You were in love with Catherine Neale?"

"In love with," he agreed. "Married to."

"*What?*"

He smiled wryly. "It was a long time ago. We were both nobodies. I was in New York working for Camilo. You know who he was?"

Chloe did. Camilo was a god in the photography pantheon—one of the premier "people" photographers of the last half of the twentieth century. He had also been, if she remembered the gossip right, Catherine Neale's husband.

"You stole Catherine Neale from Camilo?"

Gib shook his head. A corner of his mouth lifted slightly. "He stole Catherine from me."

Chloe stared at him. "Stole her from *you*?"

"I was working for Camilo. And Cat wanted Camilo to take her picture. She had this notion that if he did, she'd get noticed. I was her way in. I was a stupid, naive kid from Iowa in the big city for the first time. What did I know?"

There was a hint of bitterness and a whole lot of rueful self-recognition in his words—and they were words Chloe found hit pretty close to her home, too. "Like me," she said softly.

He nodded. "Like you. It was one of the reasons I didn't want you there. I could see that what had happened to me could easily happen to you. You were as big an innocent as I was. I couldn't protect my own innocence. How the hell could I protect yours?"

Chloe wrapped her fingers around his and held on tightly. It looked very different now—how he'd reacted to her in the beginning. It made her grateful to him. It made her love him all the more.

She told him so.

He looked at her. "I didn't do anything very lovable. I tried to get rid of you. And not just for your own safety. I was protecting myself, too."

"I was getting under your skin?" Chloe smiled.

"You could say that," Gib said gruffly.

Her smile widened. "Good." Then she cocked her head. "Gina didn't tell me you'd been married."

"Gina never knew."

"What?" Chloe stared at him, shocked.

He shrugged. "I didn't advertise the fact. We weren't married long. I went originally for the summer. I was going to come back to Collierville in the fall—to set up my own business—to try to make it photographing people—not beautiful people—real people."

"The ones in the photos in your apartment."

He nodded. "That's what I wanted. The internship with Camilo was just a way to learn from a master."

"Like me with you."

Gib snorted. "But then I met Cat and she encouraged me to stay. 'To learn,' she said. She hadn't got her photos from Camilo yet. She was busy getting mine then."

"The book?" The photos that had captured Catherine Neale in all her moods. The ones that saw directly into her heart. The photos that told as much about the photographer as about his object.

"Yeah. I was infatuated. I couldn't get enough of her. And all the while she was working at getting to him through me."

"Your photos were wonderful."

"They were painful. It was like wearing my heart on my sleeve. I didn't ever do it again."

He hadn't. She could see that. He'd very deliberately gone the other way. He'd focused on the body after that. He'd left out the soul.

"What happened finally?" Chloe asked. She knew they wouldn't speak of it again.

"I was a stepping stone. I thought she really loved me. I thought I'd work with Camilo through the fall, and then at Christmas I'd bring my wife home to meet my sister and then we'd stay right here and I'd do what I intended to do. I didn't reckon on what Cat had in mind. She said what she thought I wanted to hear. I was a fool." He shook his head and reached down to pluck at a weed. "At Thanksgiving we were invited to Camilo's. She charmed him. She teased him. She sat right there with me in the room and made a play for him. And she got her photos—and even got the man, eventually. She dumped me before Christmas, ran to Vegas with my boss, came home Mrs. Camilo Volano."

"And no one ever knew? About you and...and her?" Chloe couldn't even bring herself to say the woman's name.

"In those days no one cared about her private life. We were only married a few months. Gina was pregnant, very. Expecting Tom, and it hadn't been an easy pregnancy. I knew she couldn't come out for the wedding and I didn't want her to feel bad about missing it. So I just didn't tell her. Cat and I were in a hurry and we didn't want to make a big deal out of it, anyway. *She* didn't want to," he corrected. "And I thought I'd just surprise Gina when we went home for Christmas." He gave a bitter laugh. "But Cat had divorced me by Christmas. And it turned out the joke was on me."

"Oh, Gib!" Chloe put her arms around him. She hugged him. She kissed him. She wanted to assuage all the hurt, all the pain, all the past. "She was the fool."

He shrugged. "She was a user. And I swore no one was going to get close enough to do it again. No one has. Except you."

"I would never—"

"I know that! You're not like her at all."

Chloe grimaced. "I hope that's a compliment."

He grinned and tangled a golden curl around his finger. "It is. It's the highest praise I know." He paused, then ran his tongue over his lips and looked straight into her eyes. "It's also a proposal. Will you marry me? Will you put up with me? Will you grow old with me? I love you, Chlo'."

"Well," Chloe said, "when you put it like that..."

And then she launched herself at him again. And it was

fortunate they were still sitting on the ground because he didn't have quite so far to fall this time when she knocked him flat.

He laughed. His eyes were damp, but he laughed. "Is this a yes, Chloe mine?"

And she laughed with him, smiled down into his eyes, and promised him forever with her heart. She kissed him, long and hard, and he returned it until they were breathless.

And still he looked at her, still he waited. "Chloe?"

She gave him one more kiss—and the promise of a lifetime to go with it. "I do believe, Gibson, that it's a yes."

HARLEQUIN PRESENTS®

Seduction
SWEET REVENGE

They wanted to get even.
Instead they got...married!

by bestselling author

Penny Jordan

Don't miss Penny Jordan's latest enthralling miniseries
about four special women. Kelly, Anna, Beth and Dee
share a bond of friendship and a burning desire to
avenge a wrong. But in their quest for revenge, they
each discover an even stronger emotion.
Love.

Look out for all four books in Harlequin Presents®:

November 1999
THE MISTRESS ASSIGNMENT

December 1999
LOVER BY DECEPTION

January 2000
A TREACHEROUS SEDUCTION

February 2000
THE MARRIAGE RESOLUTION

Available at your favorite retail outlet.

HARLEQUIN®
Makes any time special ™

If you enjoyed what you just read,
then we've got an offer you can't resist!

Take 2 bestselling love stories FREE!

Plus get a FREE surprise gift!

Clip this page and mail it to Harlequin Reader Service®

IN U.S.A.	IN CANADA
3010 Walden Ave.	P.O. Box 609
P.O. Box 1867	Fort Erie, Ontario
Buffalo, N.Y. 14240-1867	L2A 5X3

YES! Please send me 2 free Harlequin Presents® novels and my free surprise gift. Then send me 6 brand-new novels every month, which I will receive months before they're available in stores. In the U.S.A., bill me at the bargain price of $3.12 plus 25¢ delivery per book and applicable sales tax, if any*. In Canada, bill me at the bargain price of $3.49 plus 25¢ delivery per book and applicable taxes**. That's the complete price and a savings of over 10% off the cover prices—what a great deal! I understand that accepting the 2 free books and gift places me under no obligation ever to buy any books. I can always return a shipment and cancel at any time. Even if I never buy another book from Harlequin, the 2 free books and gift are mine to keep forever. So why not take us up on our invitation. You'll be glad you did!

106 HEN CNER
306 HEN CNES

Name	(PLEASE PRINT)	
Address	Apt.#	
City	State/Prov.	Zip/Postal Code

* Terms and prices subject to change without notice. Sales tax applicable in N.Y.
** Canadian residents will be charged applicable provincial taxes and GST.
All orders subject to approval. Offer limited to one per household.
® are registered trademarks of Harlequin Enterprises Limited.

PRES99   ©1998 Harlequin Enterprises Limited

"This book is DYNAMITE!"
—**Kristine Rolofson**

"A riveting page turner…"
—**Joan Elliott Pickart**

"Enough twists and turns to keep everyone
guessing… What a ride!"
—**Jule McBride**

See what all your favorite authors
are talking about.

Coming October 1999 to a retail store near you.

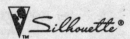

Coming Next Month

HARLEQUIN PRESENTS®

THE BEST HAS JUST GOTTEN BETTER!

#2061 THE MISTRESS ASSIGNMENT Penny Jordan
(Sweet Revenge/Seduction)
Kelly has agreed to act the seductress in order to teach a lesson to the man who betrayed her best friend. It's a scheme fraught with danger—especially when gorgeous stranger Brough Frobisher gets caught in the cross fire....

#2062 THE REVENGE AFFAIR Susan Napier
(Presents Passion)
Joshua Wade was convinced that Regan was plotting to disrupt their wedding. Regan had to admit there was unfinished business between them—a reckless one-night stand.... She had good reason for getting close to Joshua, though, but she could never reveal her secret plans....

#2063 SLADE BARON'S BRIDE Sandra Marton
(The Barons)
When Lara Stevens and Slade Baron were both facing an overnight delay in an airport, Slade suggested they spend the time together. Who would she hurt if Lara accepted his invitation? He wanted her, and she wanted . . . his child!

#2064 THE BOSS'S BABY Miranda Lee
(Expecting!)
When Olivia's fiancé ditched her, her world had been blown apart and with it, her natural caution. She'd gone to the office party and seduced her handsome boss! But now Olivia has a secret she dare not tell him!

#2065 THE SECRET DAUGHTER Catherine Spencer
Soon after Joe Donnelly's sizzling night with Imogen Palmer, she'd fled. Now ten years on, Joe was about to uncover an astonishing story—one that would culminate in a heartrending reunion with the daughter he never knew he had.

#2066 THE SOCIETY GROOM Mary Lyons
(Society Weddings)
When Olivia meets her former lover, rich socialite Dominic FitzCharles, at a society wedding, he has a surprise for her: he announces their betrothal to the press, in front of London's elite. Just how is Olivia supposed to say no?